Bedtime Stories
for Lovers

II

Bedtime Stories for Lovers II

JOAN ELIZABETH LLOYD

BOOKSPAN
GARDEN CITY, NEW YORK

Book club edition published by Bookspan,
401 Franklin Avenue, Garden City, New York

Copyright © 2000 by Joan E. Lloyd

ISBN: 0-7394-1142-x

Design by Paul Randall Mize

Contents

Contents

An Introduction

I love a good erotic short story, one that allows me to explore my more adventurous side or one that delves into my romantic nature. Whether it's a fairy tale like those in my first collection, *Bedtime Stories for Lovers,* or one of the more contemporary ones here, it tells of lovers playing, reveling in creativity.

Here are more than twenty of my favorites, stories I've written over the last few years. Whether it's the dark, delicious world of "Music" or the true fantasy world of "Blind Passion," all of these stories are fun to read and even more fun to bring into your bedroom. Read them privately or with your lover. If there's a story here that makes you smile, that curls your toes, or that piques your sexual curiosity, don't keep that a secret. If you don't feel brave enough to read it to your lover, slip a bookmark in it and put it into your partner's briefcase or lunch box. He or she will certainly understand, and you'll both benefit from your bravery.

Erotica is so personal that you might find a story or two in this collection that you don't enjoy. Skip any tale that you don't like, and go on to the next. I know there will be many that you will want to read again and again.

So let's begin.

Bedtime Stories for Lovers

II

for Lovers

The Cave

of Delight

*I*T WAS SPOKEN OF around the village, but only in whispers. Bret had heard about the Cave of Delight from his older brothers, not as fact but as something young men fantasized about. No one would admit to having searched for it, but everyone knew that in the twilight boys from the surrounding area wandered through the woods and searched at the foot of the nearby mountains. No one had ever found it, at least not that anyone knew.

The Cave of Delight. All one's sexual fantasies came true inside. The most beautiful women would do anything to make you happy. But, according to the rumors, you could stay for only one night, after which you could never return. It would be a night worth whatever it cost, and Bret would pay any price.

So Bret searched. Every evening after working in his

father's fields, he would take off in a different direction and walk until it got dark, then find his way home by the light of the lantern he carried. And occasionally he didn't return until morning. No one noticed, and he was completely at home out in the open.

One afternoon he finished his plowing, and, with a sack containing his lantern, a loaf of bread, and a small wheel of cheese, he took off in a new direction. Soon he would marry, he thought. The match had been arranged for him by his family, and he hadn't yet seen the woman. It didn't matter. Marriage was for bearing children—strong sons to work in the fields, beautiful daughters to help their mother and eventually marry into powerful families. Good loving? Bret sighed. He hoped so and would do whatever he could to make it so, but from what he knew of his married friends and brothers, it was usually rather ordinary. It would be comfortable sex every evening if he wanted.

As the shadows lengthened and the air cooled, he kept walking toward faraway hills. Suddenly he saw a rabbit disappear behind some rocks. Realizing that he'd never been aware of anything behind the small rockfall, he followed the rabbit. Finding a small passageway, he wiggled through the narrow opening and crawled through a low tunnel.

He heard water running and felt warm air on his face, and he kept crawling. Finally the tunnel sloped downward and widened. When the ceiling became high enough, Bret stood up and walked, ending up in a small cave. He looked around in the dim light, his eyes barely able to make out the rock walls and the small pool at the foot of a low waterfall. How could he see at all in a completely enclosed cave? Where was the faint illumination coming from? He shook his head and set his pack on a ledge.

He walked to the edge of the pool and dipped his fingers in the water. Rather than the cold of the springs near the farm, this water was almost hot. Again he looked around. Nothing but rock. He realized he was hot and sweaty and thought a dip in the warm spring would feel wonderful. He quickly stripped off his clothes and walked into the water. In the center, the water came up to his shoulders so he lifted his feet and floated on the smooth surface.

"I didn't think you'd be able to swim," a soft voice said.

Bret stood up and looked around the inside of the cave but saw no one. "Who's there?" Nothing. He must have imagined the voice, but it had sounded so clear. After a few moments, the lifted his feet and put his head back, lifting his hips to the surface.

"Very beautiful," she said.

Suddenly he realized that he was naked, and he stood so the water concealed his body. "Okay, stop fooling around. Who's there?"

Her laugh was musical, and he knew that he'd never heard anything like it before. "Me," she said.

Again Bret stood up. "And who's me?"

"You can call me Marie." There was a splash and he felt, rather than saw, a presence in the pool. Her head surfaced beside his, and he got a dim look at his companion. Although he couldn't see her very well, he knew that she was beautiful. He couldn't tell what color her long wet hair was nor could he see her eyes clearly, but her skin was like ivory, her neck long. She stood beside him, and she was almost as tall as he was.

"I just found this cave," Bret said, "but I guess you've known about it for a while."

"Oh yes. I come here often." She ducked beneath the warm water, and he felt her hair brush against his flank as she swam below the surface. He reached down and grabbed at her and felt bare, soft flesh. Her buttocks? Was she as naked as he was?

She surfaced, and her musical laugh filled the cave. "So, you want to play." Again she dove, and he felt hands on his thigh. Shaking his head, he, too, dove beneath the water and reached for anything he could touch. Her body was indeed naked, and his hands found her breasts and her ankles.

For long minutes, they dove, surfaced, laughed, and dove again, until Bret was breathless. Finally the two stood side by side in the water, panting. "You are very handsome," she said when she could breathe easily again.

"And you are very beautiful," he said.

Then her lips were against his, and the length of her lush body pressed his. Her hand cupped his head as the kiss lengthened. This wasn't play anymore, and his body knew it. He was hard and her hand found him, circling his erection with long fingers.

When he groaned, she laughed, her joy obvious. "Wonderful," she said, holding him under the warm water. She cupped his balls and touched the tender spot just in front of his anus. He reached for her and held her breasts, stroking the soft skin, teasing her hard nipples.

"You must stop," he said.

"But why?" she asked.

"You don't know what will happen if you continue."

"Of course I do, silly. And it will be magnificent. I know." She continued to knead his hardness, forcing him to concentrate on not spurting yet. This was too fantastic. Her hands felt so good touching him, and her breasts filled his hands. He slid his palms around to her back, then down to cup her buttocks. He lifted her, and she wrapped her thighs around his waist.

He pushed her upward and, as her head fell backward, took one turgid nipple in his mouth. He suckled, listening to her moans of pleasure, trying to extend their tender lovemaking. But he knew his body would wait no longer. He lowered her slowly along the length of his chest and was inside her with one smooth thrust, the water cushioning his movements. In perfect rhythm they matched their motions as his erection slid in and out of her slick passage. It was going to be too quick, he knew, as he felt his orgasm boiling in his belly. His fingers found her clit and he rubbed, trying to increase her obvious pleasure.

"Oh yes," she screamed, and he felt small spasms ripple through her channel. His back arched, and too soon he erupted deep inside of her.

He didn't make it home that night. They stayed together in the cave, sharing his bread and cheese and making love many more times. Finally she told him that he would have to leave. "I don't want to go," he moaned.

"I know, but you have to. You are allowed only one night."

"This is the Cave of Delight?" he gasped.

"I thought you knew," she said.

He was desolate. But he knew where the opening of the cave was, so he could find it again. He would. "I hadn't thought about it, but I want to return."

"I know, but it is impossible."

Slowly he put his clothes back on, determined to come back that very night. He kissed her good-bye, and, as he crawled back through the tunnel, he heard her magical laugh.

He returned to the rocks that night, but there was

no opening, no tunnel, no cave. Night after night he combed the rocks but, alas, no cave.

Months later, he was resigned to his marriage. Maybe she'd be more than he expected, yet she could never be Marie. Never.

Two days before his wedding, he traveled to his future wife's village with his parents and his eldest brother. When they arrived at her family's farm, he was seated in the small main room, and he watched as she slowly glided down the stairs. She was quite lovely, with long auburn hair and soft, white skin. "My name is Jane," she said, "but my friends call me by my middle name, Marie."

"Marie?" he said, pained by the coincidence.

"Yes," she said, lowering her eyes. "You can call me Jane if you prefer."

He had to forget the night in the cave. It was a fantasy, and this was reality. "Of course I will call you Marie."

"And you are Bret. I like that name."

They talked for a few minutes, then were called into the dining room for dinner. She went into the kitchen to help with the serving, and suddenly he heard her musical laugh. It was her laugh, the angel from the cave. She walked from the kitchen, still laughing. It was her. There could be no mistake. As she sat beside him, he whispered, "It was you, wasn't it?"

"It was the cave of your delight, what you wanted most. Many have been there, and each gets what he most desires. You wanted a lover and a wife in one."

"But how?"

"I do not know, and you must not reveal any of what happened or it will disappear. Just be content that we can have our desires for the rest of our lives."

Bret couldn't control his grin. He was the happiest and luckiest of men.

The Model

JUSTIN LAY stretched out on his bed with the most recent copy of the Geneva Toy Company catalog propped on his stomach. He stared at the model clothed only in a sheer stretchy black cat suit with a pattern of vines, roses, and leaves woven in. Her well-developed breasts were clearly defined beneath the lacy fabric. He sighed and traced her outline with his index finger. "I'd really love to play with that," he whispered.

"And so you shall," a woman's voice sighed into his ear.

"Yeah, right," he growled. "Now I'm hearing voices."

"No, you aren't. You're hearing me."

Justin sat up and looked around. There was nothing out of the ordinary in his room. "Hearing who?" he asked. "Where the hell are you?"

"Right here," the voice said, seeming to come from the foot of his bed.

"Right where?"

"Here."

Justin stared at the place from which the voice seemed to be coming. The air appeared to shimmer, like when you drive down a road in the summer and you see the heat rising off the pavement. The air became somehow less transparent, as though seeing his dresser through a gauzy curtain. "What the fuck's going on here?"

"Just be patient. You have to be patient."

The air thickened, and slowly a shape began to appear. There was a torso, then legs. Long, shapely legs that seemed to rise forever from a pair of black, high-heeled shoes. The torso solidified, and soft breasts, a flat belly, and narrow hips were visible. Shoulders appeared, with long arms, then hands with long fingernails polished bright red. A head formed from a small plume of hazy smoke, the face smiling, the hair wild and black. As she became a woman, he realized that she was indeed the model from the catalog, dressed in the lacy, black cat suit in the picture.

"Just a few moments more," she said as her body thickened and became three dimensional. "It takes less and less time each time I do this."

"Excuse me?"

"I've learned to materialize when a man wishes for me. And you did."

"I did?" Justin was totally bemused. What was happening? Was he losing his mind? This kind of thing just didn't happen. Not to sane men. He raked his fingers through his shoulder-length brown hair.

"Yes. You said, and I quote, 'I'd like to play with that.' End quote. I distinctly heard you. *So*, here I am so you can play."

"Play?"

"Listen, buster, stop asking silly questions. You sound like the village idiot. And I've known my share, believe me."

Justin took a deep breath. "Okay. I'll stop asking questions if you explain what's going on."

"I told you," she said, sounding totally exasperated, "but I'll explain it one more time. You wished for me. I materialized. Sort of like the genie in the lamp, except you rubbed my body. Now I'm yours to play with. Do what you want with." She reached over and grabbed Justin's cock through the crotch of his jeans. "And I'll bet I know just what you want."

Justin almost said Do anything?, but he thought one more question might make her disappear again. He looked her over carefully from head to foot, and he had to agree that he wanted to play with that. She was a perfect sex object, and the cat suit brought out both her best features. And great features they were. He reached out and touched the tip of one breast with the end of his index finger. His finger met warm, firm flesh.

Her laugh was deep and throaty. "No, your hand doesn't pass right through me. I'm real. Flesh and blood." She stepped back and placed her hands on her hips. "And not bad flesh it is, too." She turned left and right, modeling, showing off her fantastic body.

"Not bad at all," Justin said. "And it's really mine to play with?"

"All yours. What would you like?"

Oh God, he thought, what would he like? Everything. In his twenty-eight years, he'd never had an offer like that. Everything. Where to start? "How long do I have you for?"

"For now. The rest kind of works itself out." She cupped her breasts through the lacy black material of the cat suit. "Want to start here?"

"Oh yes," Justin said and cupped both palms over her magnificent breasts. He felt the nipples come alive in his hands as his fingers kneaded and squeezed. "Not too hard," she said. "Wouldn't want to bruise the merchandise."

"Sorry," Justin said. "Why don't you come here and sit beside me?"

She sat on the edge of the bed and, as Justin's hand continued to caress her breasts, unbuttoned his shirt. "Umm," she purred. "Nice. I'm not overly fond of big hairy chests. Yours is smooth and so good to touch." She ran her hands over his skin, touching all the places Justin loved to be touched. Her fingers were almost electric, causing shivers down his back. "Maybe you'd like me to take this off," she said, pulling at his shirt. He moved so his arms pulled out of the sleeves. "Yes," she purred. "Nice."

"And maybe you'd like to take that outfit off, too."

"Oh no." She fiddled with the front of the garment and soon two of the intricate leaves that had appeared to grow from the vines on the suit were in her hand. "These seem to be part of the pattern, but they really come off. See?"

He did see. The leaves that she had removed exposed her large deep brown nipples. "Very convenient." He pinched her swollen tips, causing them to get harder and tighter. "Very convenient."

She tugged at Justin's belt. "I thought you'd think so. It's for sale, but more of that later. How about taking this off?" she purred.

Justin needed no urging. His cock was so swollen that his pants had become terribly uncomfortable. What the hell? He stood, quickly pulled off his jeans and shorts. Now naked, he sat back down on the bed, his cock sticking straight up from his groin like a flagpole. "That's so big," she purred. "Can I touch it?"

Justin was afraid that if she touched his cock, he'd go off right then. What the hell? "Sure. Touch away."

She seemed to know exactly what he wanted. She wrapped her hand around his stiff cock and pushed down, then rubbed the tightened skin over the tip with the fingers of her other hand. She trapped the head of his cock in her hand, pressed down, and, as the head pushed through her tightened fingers, her other hand grasped it. Justin was in heaven.

"This would work better with some Geneva Lube," she said, and almost instantly a tube of slippery stuff appeared in her hand. She squeezed a big glob in her palm and went back to work, rubbing his cock. He was trembling with the excitement of it all, but he wasn't quite to the point of coming. It was as though she knew how to keep him just below his peak.

"Would you like me to lick it?" she asked, her voice soft and sensuous.

"Oh God," Justin groaned, dropping onto his back and spreading his legs.

"How about some Geneva-flavored gel?" she said and, as if by magic, a jar had appeared and she was spreading some on his cock. The scent of chocolate filled his nostrils. "It comes in strawberry and banana, too."

She sounded kind of like a commercial, but when

her mouth enveloped his cock, he forgot everything else. Her mouth was amazing, as talented on his cock as her hand had been. She lay the flat of her tongue against the underside of his cock, then pulled her head back with just enough suction. Her tongue flicked the tip and swirled around the head. God, she was good. It felt as if he were soaring.

"Are you ready to fuck me?" she said a while later.

"Absolutely." If her pussy was as great as her hands and mouth, he was in for the best fuck of his life.

"A Geneva tickler," she said, unrolling a condom over his cock. "See," she added, "it has a little thingie on the end that unrolls when you come inside of me. Actually, I've never felt anything, but it's supposed to be the best so I always use one."

Before he had time to react, she straddled his hips and lowered her hot pussy onto his cock. "See how convenient," she said. "The suit has no crotch so I can do this very easily."

Her hot pussy surrounded his cock, and she raised and lowered her body, fucking him expertly. "Good?"

"Oh God," he groaned, trying not to come. Make it last, he vowed, but it was no use. He climaxed almost immediately.

"That was really good," she said only moments later. "I have some Geneva towelettes here." She pulled off the condom and used the cool towel to clean his cock

and balls. "See? All nice and clean. These are really use-
ful for those away-from-the-bedroom fucks."

"Yeah," Justin moaned. "Convenient."

"Okay. How many would you like?"

"Huh?" Justin's fuzzy mind tried to understand what
she was saying.

"How many? Or would you like a dozen of the tickler condoms. They're on sale this week."

"Okay, I'm gone. What's going on?"

"I was just trying to take your order."

"Order?"

"Sure. The cat suit's only forty-nine ninety-five. Or
you might want to order the lube or the gel."

"But I don't want to order anything."

"So why were you looking at the catalog?" she asked,
a bit bemused.

"I just like to look at your picture. And all the other
girls, too."

"You don't want to order anything?"

"No. Not really."

"Nothing?"

"Nothing."

"Well then, it's been fun."

Slowly her body began to dissolve. "Wait," Justin
said. "I don't get it."

"If you don't buy anything, you don't get the ordering service," she said. "Bye."

"But wait—"

"No order, no service. Sorry." And she was gone.

Justin stared at the spot where she had been, then picked up the catalog and gazed. Then he stroked the model's picture. "I'd really like to play with that," he said. But she never reappeared.

The Monica Thing

HALLOWEEN had never been one of her favorite holidays, but as Linda surveyed the swirling mass of humanity, she realized that this party was going to be a real bummer. Halloween. Almost as commercial now as Christmas. People in her neighborhood had hung orange lights around their windows, for God's sake. This whole thing was crazy.

She had taken out her frustration with the holiday on her costume. Monica. Blue dress and black wig with a jaunty black beret set at a rakish angle. And a rubber mask that covered her face down to the mouth. She looked down. The dress even had a small stain in what she assumed was the right place. What a joke.

And this party. Too loud, too frantic, too . . . well just too. But she had promised her friend Val that she would attend, so attend she would. She had said her good evenings to Val, and hopefully, without too much notice, she'd slip out again after as short a time as possible, go home, and watch TV.

"Would you do it?" a voice said in her ear. She spun to see a Bill Clinton just behind her. He wore a well-tailored blue suit, wing tip shoes, and a rubber mask that covered most of his face. He was tall, his body lean, but she could make out little more than that and the fact that his eyes were brown.

"I'm sorry. Would I do what?"

"Give Bill Clinton head."

"Not a chance. I'm a devout Republican. I'd probably bite it off."

"I wouldn't like that," the man said, putting his hand on her arm, "but judging from the gorgeous sexy mouth of yours, you'd be great doing the Monica thing."

"Would you let me?"

"Okay, now I'm confused."

"Would you let someone you didn't know get her teeth that close to your prized possession?"

His laughter was spontaneous and genuine. "I don't suppose I would. But then in a few minutes we wouldn't be strangers, would we?" He smiled down at her. "Drink?"

A few moments ago she'd been planning her escape, but now she nodded. "I'd love a white wine."

"A Monica drink if there ever was one." He turned toward the bar. "Don't disappear."

"Would Monica do that to Bill?" Linda answered.

And she waited, amazed and exhilarated. She had no clue what the guy looked like or what kind of a person he was, but somehow she liked him. And he had sexy hands. She caught herself up short. Where had that thought come from? Well, I'm just being honest. He does have great hands. She had noticed his long, nicely shaped fingers as he had briefly held her arm. She was a sucker for sexy hands.

And that hand now held out a glass of white wine. "Let's go out onto the terrace," he said. "It's much quieter there, and maybe we can talk. Discuss politics, my being a Democrat and all."

Although it was the last night of October, the air was just warm enough to relax outside without getting chilled. They stood and talked for a while as they sipped their drinks. The talk never got personal enough for them to learn much about each other, but they laughed a lot and Linda felt charmed and completely comfortable. As she leaned on the railing, she shivered a bit.

"Chilly?" Bill asked, moving behind her. He wrapped his arms around her, his hands just beneath her breasts. "I have a great idea about how to warm you up, Monica."

This was moving much too fast, Linda thought, but his arms felt so good. His thumbs began to rub the undersides of her breasts, and she felt her body responding. This is nuts, she told herself. I don't know this guy's name or even what he looks like beneath that mask. Yet, I'm letting him touch me, and I'm enjoying it. Her Monica dress buttoned up the front, and she felt his fingers undo the buttons then his warm, sexy hands slip inside. As his fingers cupped her breasts, she allowed her head to fall back against his shoulder.

She didn't realize just how quickly things were moving until he flipped open the clasp at the front of her bra, then suddenly his hands were on her bare breasts. Her breasts, and particularly her nipples, had always been her downfall. Several of her ex-boyfriends had discovered that and taken advantage of her weakness, touching, biting, pinching until she was moaning, and she willingly accepted anything they wanted to do with her.

His fingers were pinching her nipples, making heat lance down her body to her groin. She felt herself opening, moistening, readying herself for him. Oh God, she couldn't help responding to him.

And what would be the harm. He didn't have a clue who she was, and she didn't know him. A quick fling, then anonymity. What's the problem? She mentally shook her head. No problem.

Her back was still against his chest, and her buttocks detected how excited he was becoming as well. Hard, fully erect male flesh, only thinly covered by his Bill Clinton suit pants pressed into her cheeks. A soft moan escaped her lips. She was still looking over the city when one of his hands slid down and grabbed the front of her skirt. Slowly he lifted and pulled until his hand could grasp the front of her panties and slip inside. With one of his hands still kneading her breast and one rubbing her mound, she moaned. "Oh yes," he whispered. "Yes. So wet." He seemed to know just where to rub, touch, invade, and she tipped her pelvis so his fingers could slide into her channel. She wanted. Now!

She reached down and grabbed his hand, pressing the heel into her clit. She rubbed her body against his hand and arm like a cat in heat, until, with a small cry, she came. God, waves of pure pleasure rocked her. He grasped his wrist so tightly she wondered whether she would cut off the circulation. But she didn't care. She just needed.

It was long moments until the spasms subsided. "Oh God, baby," he moaned in her ear. "So incredibly responsive. I've never met anyone like you."

Linda caught her breath, then turned. "You asked me a question a while ago. I said I was a Republican." Her hands went to his zipper, and she slowly lowered it, feeling the huge mass of hardened cock beneath. "Would you trust a Republican?" As she worked his cock free of his clothing, she glanced around. Thankfully the terrace was empty. She slipped to her knees and wrapped her hand around the base of his turgid member. Knowing she wasn't able to take too much of him she wrapped her hand around the base of his hard prick, made an O with her mouth, and slowly sucked him inside. She had too active a gag reflex to do a deep throat, but her hand worked its magic. As she sucked on the end of his cock, she worked her hand rhythmically, squeezing her fingers in a pattern from her index finger on the base to her pinky about halfway up the shaft.

She knew he was close so she worked one finger in through his fly and rubbed his balls. He came with a loud groan, semen filling her mouth and making a fresh stain on her blue Monica dress.

She stood up and watched as he struggled to get his breath. What had she done? This was unthinkable. She wouldn't have dreamed of doing anything like this except for the costume. It was a Monica thing. Suddenly she was so embarrassed she wanted to slip into the house and disappear. She wasn't like this. She wasn't.

"Can I get you another glass of wine?" he asked.

"Thanks," she managed to say.

He walked into the living room, and quickly Linda slipped in behind him. She worked her way to the bedroom, grabbed her coat, and rushed out the front door. Almost running down the stairs, she pulled off her mask. What kind of a slut does he think I am? It doesn't matter, she told herself. He doesn't know who I am. She sighed. And it's really too bad. We made each other laugh a lot. Under other circumstances . . .

She tossed and turned all night, and, by eight the next morning, thankfully a Sunday, she was up, dressed, and sitting in her tiny kitchen, cradling a cup of coffee in her hands. When the phone rang just after nine, she slowly picked it up. "Hello?"

"Don't hang up, Monica, and don't be upset." He spoke quickly, getting the words out before she could think. "It's Bill. Last evening was wonderful, but much too fast. I didn't mean to behave like that, but I guess I just got carried away. Maybe if we had a regular date, without masks, we could begin again. Think about it. Please."

It was all Linda could do not to drop the phone. She cleared her throat as all that had happened rushed through her mind, heating her body. She whispered, "Last evening should be forgotten."

"Last evening should be remembered and savored. It was sensational. And my name's Greg."

Linda hesitated. "How did you get my number?"

"I hounded Val until she gave it to me. She wouldn't give me your name and made me promise that I would forget the number if you weren't interested. Please. Give us a chance."

Linda couldn't help it. It was impossible not to smile. He was so sweet, and it had been so wonderful. "Okay," she said. "Hi, Greg. My name's Linda."

The Perfect Mate

THERE WAS ONCE a princess named Tamara who had bullied her father into agreeing that she wouldn't have to marry anyone who wasn't her perfect mate. Over the past two years she had met and rejected seventeen princes, twenty-two noblemen, two sheiks from faraway kingdoms, and even several commoners. No one was handsome enough, tall enough, wise enough, witty enough. No one was good enough for Tamara, and she didn't even give them any time to impress her. No one was her perfect mate, and her father, the king, lamented that she might never marry.

One afternoon Tamara was practicing her serve on the royal tennis court, dressed in rags. She was a very good tennis player, but she wasn't sure just how good she really was because the members of the court always let her win. "Please," she would beg, "play your hardest. I need that."

"But your majesty . . ."

So today she was dressed as a scullery maid, stealing time from her job in the kitchen. "Aren't you worried about being caught?" a voice said.

"Caught?" she asked, gazing at the stranger. He was just her height, with thick glasses, a slightly balding head, and travel-worn clothes.

"Yes. Taking time from your duties in the kitchen must be a punishable offense."

"Oh. Yes. Well, I have a few minutes. Do you play?"

"A bit," the stranger said. "But I don't think I can play here. Isn't it for royalty only?"

"I'm playing here," Tamara said. "My name's Tammy."

"Hi Tammy. I'm Kurt." They shook hands, and he continued, "I'm a stable hand, new to the court. I'd love to play, but I've no racket."

Tamara got him a racket from the collection beside the court, then proceeded to be humiliated by his powerful serve and stinging backhand. Although her feelings were hurt, she couldn't help but admire his skill. As they walked to the side of the court, sweating and panting, he winked at her. "Good game."

Winded, she winked back. "Yes, a great game. Thanks."

"I particularly liked looking at your legs when you served."

Slightly flustered, Tamara blushed. "Thank you, but you're very forward."

"Not as forward as I'd like to be," he said, a wide grin splitting his face.

Tamara had never come anywhere close to the heady feeling of flirting with a stranger who knew nothing about her. "What would you do then, sir?"

"I'd tell you how beautiful your breasts look through that blouse. I couldn't help but watch them jiggle, and it almost cost me several points."

Blushing furiously, Tamara said, "You say the most outrageous things."

"And do the most outrageous things, too," he said. Then he placed his hands on her waist and pulled her against him. Slowly his lips descended until she could feel his warm breath on her mouth. He's going to kiss me, she realized, and I'm looking forward to it.

And he did. His mouth covered hers, softly at first, then more fiercely as he adjusted the kiss to take full pleasure in her mouth. As he held her more tightly, she felt her knees weaken and her heart pound. Her rapid breathing had nothing to do with their recent exercise. She realized that her hands were pressed against his heaving chest, and she slowly slid her palms up his shirt to cup the back of his head. As she threaded her fingers through his hair, she felt his grip tighten still more and his knee press against her legs.

Without even being aware, she parted her thighs and allowed his thigh to press between them. Finally, long moments later, Kurt leaned back. "You certainly know how to kiss," he said. "Why don't we meet later in the stable and continue this in private?"

Could she? Should she? Absolutely not! "Yes," she sighed. "An hour after dinner."

Was she crazy? she wondered as she finished her evening meal. She wouldn't let him take real liberties, but she had enjoyed his kiss and wanted . . . Wanted what? She didn't really know, but she needed to find out. Although she changed her mind several times, an hour after the meal ended she found herself in the stables.

The large room was lit only by a single lantern at the far end and was redolent with the smells of hay, horse, and leather. "I didn't think you'd come," his voice said from behind her.

"I didn't think so either," she answered honestly.

Then he was against her, pressing his chest to her back, his arms around her waist, his lips nibbling at the back of her neck. "Mmm," he purred, the vibrations transmitting to her very bones.

His hands wandered to her breasts, cupping her, squeezing her, and she felt her knees tremble and her private area getting wet. When he lightly pinched one nipple, she almost passed out from the pleasure of it. "Oh gracious," she gasped.

His lips roamed her neck and shoulders, and his hands kneaded her flesh until she felt a bubble growing in her belly. Then one hand traveled down her abdomen until he found her mound. He rubbed, pressing her spine against his belly. She reveled in the feel of his hand and his obvious hardness against her buttocks. She tried to keep still and just feel, but she couldn't keep her hips from rubbing against him.

"Oh, you wanton wench," he groaned, moving them into the darker recesses of one of the stalls. "You're such a sexy thing." His fingers pressed her skirt against her groin, and he rubbed, finding her hard clit. The sensations were muffled through the layers of fabric, but she moved so the rubbing was in the exact right spot.

"Oh," she moaned. "Oh." Something grew inside of her, coloring the dim room in bright oranges and blues, swirling before her closed eyes. As his talented fingers delved more deeply between her legs, the colors exploded, wild blasts of bright reds and yellows, flying outward like fireworks. Her knees collapsed, yet his hands held her up, her back pressed against his chest.

"You're amazing," he whispered. He turned her around. "Now help me." He loosened his britches and released his erection.

Tamara had seen animals, but never a man. But he was magnificent, even in the very weak light. He guided her hand to him, and, hesitantly she touched him. Hard, yet like the smoothest, softest fabric. Warm, with a small drop of fluid oozing from the tip. "How?" she whispered.

He showed her, wrapped her fingers around him and covered her hand with his. Then he rubbed her hand along the length of his hardness, pressing her tips of her fingers into his flesh. "Faster," he groaned. "Yes. Like that."

In only a moment she felt his hips buck and suddenly thick, milky liquid spurted from the end of his prick. "Oh, God," he grunted, panting. "Magnificent."

For a long time they stood, leaning against the wall of the stall. "Tammy, I must see you again."

"And I need you, too," she said.

They cleaned up, then, hand in hand, they walked to the more brightly lit end of the stable. "You look familiar," Kurt said. "And your clothes." He looked her over. "You're not a kitchen worker, are you?"

"Well . . ."

"Oh shit . . . I know who you are. I saw you from a distance when I first got here. You're the princess."

"Yes. That's true."

"But then there's no future for us," he lamented.

"That's not necessarily true. Not true at all. Actually, I'd like to get to know you better. You just might be perfect."

Blind Passion

*I*T WAS PITCH BLACK in her room as Maria was jarred awake by the feeling of hands on her wrists. Efficiently someone tied her arms to the headboard of the bed, and quickly a blindfold was secured over her eyes. As her panic increased, a soft hand stroked her forehead. "Do not be alarmed. I understand that this all feels very scary, but I want only pleasure for you."

Maria tried to concentrate on the calm, soothing voice, but despite the reassurances, her heart pounded and her breathing accelerated. The hand was so relaxing, gently caressing her temples and then her cheeks, but her arms couldn't move and she couldn't see. "Wh-what do you want?" she managed to say, her voice squeaky and quavering.

"Only your pleasure, as I told you. Please, try to relax. I assure you that it will be wonderful."

She tried not to cry. "Why have you assaulted me like this?"

"Assaulted? No. Never. We have our reasons for needing you like this. I want to say that you should trust me, but I know you cannot."

"Trust you?" Maria almost shrieked. "Trust you?" Her laugh was almost hysterical, yet the hand on her face continued to soothe.

"I know," the man said. "I understand. It will take some time for you to accept that I mean you no harm."

Maria tried to quell the panic inside her. She was bound and blindfolded . . . yet comforted somehow. It made no sense. She felt the covers pulled off the bed, and she realized that the man could see her body through the short baby-doll pajama top she wore. "You are truly lovely," the man said. "It will be a pleasure to make you come alive."

"Come alive?" What the hell did that mean?

"Just try to relax as I said. You will soon understand everything."

What was there to understand? She was helpless, incapable of resisting anything he wanted to do to her. The hand stroking her face was so soft, caressing, but she couldn't succumb. She couldn't allow herself to relax and be raped. That was surely what was going to happen. Rape. By some unknown, unseen stranger.

Maria had always had rape fantasies, but this wasn't a fantasy, this was a real, disgusting assault. Yet the hand was so soft and was joined by a second one, touching her fingers and her palms as they were held incapable of moving in their bindings.

"I am so sorry it has to be like this," he said. "I know it is so frightening." He sighed, and somehow Maria almost felt sorry for him.

"Why are you doing this?" she asked. "You say you're sorry that it has to be like this, so don't do it."

"I am afraid it has to be," he said, his voice sounding almost sad. "But in the end, you will see how wonderful it will be."

Then Maria felt a soft kiss on her forehead, gentle, feather-soft like a mother's good-night kiss. The hands and the mouth combined to make her feel treasured, cosseted. As the lips neared her mouth, she almost parted her lips to receive the loving kiss. But she couldn't. This was so horrible.

Yet it wasn't really. How could she be of two minds like this, her brain screamed. You're being raped, yet somehow she felt that it was an act of love. "Just enjoy it," he said. "You have no choice, after all, so you might as well."

He had a point. Since she had no choices, why not just roll with things and see what happened? She should try to gather data for the police. She couldn't see anything, but what did she hear, or smell. She could stop fighting the inevitable and just go with it. She relaxed the muscles in her arms. Yes, she wouldn't fight, just gather information.

"Oh yes," he said, "that is so much better."

Learn. "Do you have a name?" Did he have an accent of some kind? That would be helpful.

"You can call me Joe." There were faint rustling sounds, and she felt him settle onto the bed beside her. "I would like to kiss you, but only when you are ready." He stroked a finger over her closed lips.

She felt her mouth open, almost of its own volition, and his finger touched her teeth. No one in her sexual past had ever been so tender, so loving. She'd been with lots of men, after all. She was almost twenty-five. But this was a first. Too bad she couldn't give in to it all. Could she? No. She was just finding out all the information she could. Right? Lips brushed hers, tentative yet sensual. She let out a long, low sigh, slowly flowing into the embrace. And it was better than any kiss she had ever had. This guy's a great kisser, she thought as her mind fuzzed. His tongue tentatively touched hers, tasting and learning what pleased her. Giving. She could no more help returning the magical kiss than she could stop breathing. She angled her head to better taste him in return, and his gentle hands cupped her face then tangled in her hair.

On and on. The kiss continued and quickly became her whole world. Was this wrong? It couldn't be. Not something so beautiful. The mouth began to wander, to her neck, her ears, her shoulders. He licked and caressed her throat and the tender hollow at the base.

He slid his tongue down the pulse in her neck, and Maria felt it quicken, not in fear but in erotic enjoyment.

"Oh," she moaned, unable to control the feelings of pleasure as Joe's mouth found all the places that made her want. His mouth kissed its way down her breastbone as his hands caressed her sides. She heard a ripping sound, then her pajamas were gone.

"So lovely," Joe said.

She wasn't, and she knew it. She was almost thirty pounds overweight and was so afraid of the sun that she was pasty white all over. She knew that her saggy breasts were large, and that's what usually attracted the men she dated, and slowly, as they got to know her, not only did they want her body, but they genuinely liked her. But beautiful? Not!

A finger pressed against her lips. "A woman enjoying passion is always beautiful, so do not argue."

She sighed and swallowed the words she had been about to utter.

"Your breasts are soft and so white. They almost glow in the moonlight."

Moonlight. Joe had obviously opened the drapes. She had wondered why no light came through the fabric of the blindfold, and now she understood. The room was lit only by the moon.

Soft hands stroked the soft flesh at the sides of her breasts, swirling toward her now erect nipples, yet not touching them. She heard a groan and realized that the sound had come from deep within her. Please, she screamed in her mind. Oh God, please. But she couldn't say it aloud. She couldn't admit that some rapist was giving her more pleasure than she had ever experienced before.

Then there was a mouth on her left breast, suckling at her nipple. Shards of ecstasy knifed through her, shooting from her breast to the hidden world between her legs. She felt her nether lips swell and moisten, opening for her lover. Lover? Her rapist. The rapist she wanted so desperately now.

Suddenly there was a mouth on her other breast. A second set of talented lips nursed and pulled at her nipple. There were two men. "No," she cried. "It's obscene."

The mouths continued, heedless of her protests. "No." And yet it became more and more difficult to object, the pleasure was so great.

"Yes, accept," Joe said.

But there were still two mouths suckling at her breasts so there had to be three men. Three? She couldn't think. This was some kind of gang rape. Yet . . .

Then there were hands. How many? She couldn't count and didn't care. Fingers tweaked her nipples, causing almost pain that further excited her. A mouth sucked on her toe. One nipped at the tip of her thumb. Fingers stroked the insides of her thighs, the backs of her knees, the insides of her elbows.

So many sensations she couldn't sort them out. She didn't have to. The erotic totality was richer than anything she had ever imagined. Then there were fingers stroking the deep valleys of her sopping pussy, exploring, arousing, massaging. She was flying, higher than she ever remembered. Whatever was happening, she could now focus only on her approaching climax.

A mouth found her swollen clit and sucked as a finger slowly entered her. And as the finger invaded her pussy, one slid into her mouth. The two fingers adopted the same rhythm, fucking her in two places at once, while a mouth sucked on her clit and one suckled at each breast.

It was too much, and she came. Hard and long, spasms rocked her, tightening every muscle in her body. As she came, there was a sound like heavy moaning from the men in the room, a deep moan that she could almost feel through her body. It was so intense and lasting, it was several minutes before she could think. Were they going to fuck her now? Did she want that? "Oh my God," she moaned.

Now she could hear deep breathing in the room. She slowly became aware of the fact that her blindfold had loosened during her writhing and now permitted her to peek out from beneath. She took a deep breath and swiveled her head to see her lovers. Were they even now pulling off their pants to complete her rape?

In the moonlight, she saw several tiny figures, only

slightly taller than the side of the bed. And from what she could make out in the shadowy moonlight, they had very large heads and tremendous eyes. They stood, still and silent, their necks craned, their faces pointed toward the ceiling. She wiggled her head against the pillow, and her blindfold came all the way off. She gasped as she realized that the men who had just done all that to her weren't human. Yet she wasn't frightened or disgusted.

"Can you explain?" she said softly.

Slowly, the creature who stood closest to her face turned and looked at her. "Oh, no," he said. "Your blindfold." It was Joe's voice.

"I can see that you're not human. Please tell me what's going on."

The creature who called himself Joe looked quickly at the others in the room, Maria couldn't tell how many. There was a soft chattering, then he turned back to her. "We may as well," he said sadly. "I am sorry you found out."

He reached over and turned on the light beside Maria's bed. In the brighter light, Maria could see that the creatures were a soft bluish color, with skin that looked slightly scaly. Except that they had almost human hands and faces. They weren't ugly, she realized, just really, really odd. "Please. Tell me. I think you owe me that."

"Yes. We do owe you much, and our gratitude as well." He sighed again. "Where we are from is too difficult to explain, so let us just say we are not from here. And we are trapped here. We landed several miles away a few of your weeks ago and have learned much from your television. It is an amazing creation."

Another of the aliens continued the story, his voice as rich and comforting as Joe's. "Our ship cannot take off again since we have too little power. But we discovered that sexual excitement, and particularly a woman's climax, creates a type of energy that we can absorb, then transfer to our ship. It is a bit difficult to explain any better than that."

A third picked up the story. As Maria looked around, she counted seven of the creatures surrounding her bed. "You are the second woman we have used like this. I am truly sorry, but we felt that we gave so much pleasure that it was not really stealing. And you do not use that energy anyway. And you were not supposed to find out who we are."

"So your plan was just to disappear afterward?"

"Yes. And it worked the first time. But you got the blindfold off. That was a mistake. We must never let anything like that happen again, of course."

"And that's why you tied my hands, too."

"Of course. Had you reached out and touched one of us, you would have known immediately."

"But you're such wonderful lovers, why don't you just tell someone. Any woman would be glad to have such talented sex partners."

"Yes, maybe. But the panic we would cause would overwhelm your planet, and we would be lost."

"Yeah. I guess you're right. It was so good. If you had asked, I would have gladly given you what you took."

The creature called Joe reached over and untied Maria's hands. "We are truly sorry. We never meant to hurt anyone."

"And you didn't. That was the best sex I've ever had." Suddenly Maria's mind was whirling, her entrepreneurial spirit rushing to the fore. "You know, we could both make out really well here." She pictured a sort of pleasure palace for women, a place where the only rules were you could not use your hands and you had to wear a blind-fold. She knew women who would pay a fortune for sexual pleasure like she had just had. And these aliens would get all the energy they could use. It might work. It just might work. "I think I've got a plan."

Blind Passion

THE NEXT CHAPTER

WHAT THE HELL am I doing here, Dena Powell thought to herself. I must be out of my mind. She heaved a sigh and acknowledged that the waiting was driving her nuts. How had she gotten herself into this?

It had all started several weeks before, in the sauna at the racquet club. She had been soaking alone in the heat when Maria Marquez walked in, wrapped in a huge yellow towel. "Maria," she had said, standing to embrace her old friend. "I haven't seen you in months. How the heck are you?"

"Dena," the taller woman said, hugging her friend. "I'm fantastic. And you?"

"Not too bad." She dropped back onto the wooden bench, lying on her belly atop her striped towel. "I'm learning."

"I heard about you and Henry," Maria said, spreading her towel on the upper shelf and stretching out on her back. "How are you holding up?"

"Surviving. It's been almost four months."

"Dating?"

"Not now. It's taking me a while to adjust."

Maria winked. "Getting any?"

Dena barked a laugh. "Not a bit. I've almost forgotten what good sex is like. I'm really not up to dating and all the rigmarole that goes with it."

"That doesn't preclude good sex, however."

"It doesn't? What's a nondating woman supposed to do, run up to some guy on the street and beg to get laid?" Dena sighed, then turned over and wiped the sweat from her body with the corner of the towel.

"Not exactly. What do men do under similar circumstances?"

"I'm not into meat markets and bar pickups. One-night stands are almost as complicated and as dangerous as dating. Not a chance."

"I wasn't referring to one-night stands. However, if men can go to prostitutes, then what about us women?"

"Dial a date? You've got to be kidding. Women don't do that sort of thing."

"And why not?"

"It's just not done. Male prostitutes? Please!"

"Not male prostitutes. Men who just want to please you. Men who know exactly what you want and how to make it good." She turned onto her stomach and looked down at her friend. "And they can."

"What do you know about it? Have you been indulging?"

"I have indeed. Actually, I've got a few guys working with me who really know what's what, and where's where. You mention what you like, and voilà. Orgasms to end all orgasms. No strings, no commitments. It's all purely therapeutic. Just to get the kinks out, so to speak."

Dena sat up and looked Maria in the eye. "You're serious."

"I sure am. I've started a business, and I've already got more than a dozen steady customers. I get a small sum each time, and the guys get what they want. Believe me, they just want to please. They are happy only if they can provide great, and I do mean *great*, sex. Actually, I guarantee the best sex you've ever had, and you pay afterward, only if you think what I've said is true." She raised an eyebrow. "Interested?"

"Not a chance."

Maria mentioned a quite reasonable dollar amount. "That's what I usually charge, but since we've known each other for so long, let me offer my friends' services to you for free. Visit one afternoon, and see what they can do for you."

"Thanks, Maria, but I don't think so."

"Sure. No problem. If you should change your

mind, give me a call. I'm still at the old number, and I'll gladly make arrangements."

Dena thought about Maria's offer for a week, getting more and more excited and more and more confused by the hour. Her body wanted it. Badly. But her mind rebelled. It's so sleazy, so dirty. She remembered her sex with Henry, the best thing about their relationship. He had been a really good, creative lover, and together they had explored many different areas of sexuality. They had spent hours seeing how many orgasms each could experience. Nothing could ever be that good again. Could it? Maria had seemed so sure.

It was almost two weeks after the afternoon in the sauna when Dena called her friend. They had talked and gotten comfortable enough for Dena to share some of the areas of passion that she particularly enjoyed. "Come over to my place at five tomorrow, and I'll set it up. There are only two rules. You will have to be blindfolded. Several of my guys don't want to be recognized, so you'll have to fantasize about who they are. Maybe Sean Penn or Kevin Sorbo. You'll never know. That's part of the deal. Second, you may not touch them, but from what you've told me, that's no problem."

"You keep talking about men, plural. I'm not sure I want more than one person."

"You have to trust me. Our magic word is 'spaceship.' If you say it at any time, everything will stop and

you can go home, no questions asked. You're completely safe. I know 'trust me' is a hackneyed phrase,
but you just have to."

So here she was, lying naked, facedown on a work-
out bench in her friend's basement. She was, as Maria
had warned her, blindfolded, and her arms and legs
were tied to the legs of the bench. Her large breasts
hung down on either side of the narrow leather
padding. And she waited.

Suddenly something rustled and she felt earphones
placed over her ears. Soft romantic music began, just
loud enough to block out any other sounds from the
room. She heard a wailing saxophone and a soft clar-
inet, sounding like a warm summer night. Now she
could neither hear nor see. Something touched her
upper lip and she smelled the scent of exotic spice. It
filled her nostrils, making her head swim. She was in
her own cocoon, surrounded by sensuality.

Suddenly something pinched her right nipple.
Something was being clipped to it, tightly, almost
painfully. There was no stroking, no kissing, no
fondling. Just the clamp on her nipple. Another clip.
Shards of pain, yet not pain rocketed through her, and
she moaned. She felt the sparks echo through her
pussy, opening her, causing moisture to flow from her
core. She felt her lips swell and her clit harden.
Muscles twitched, and her mound throbbed. She had
told Maria about her love of the combination of pain

and pleasure, a love that Henry had honed over their years together. Could anyone else bring out that part of her?

The clips on her nipples were pulled, dragging her nipples downward on either side of the bench. "Please," she said. Please what? Stop. Continue? She didn't know. She didn't care. And the melancholy saxophone wailed in her ears.

Alternate pulling and releasing had her body's responses sharpened to a fine edge. Soon she was trembling, wet and open, ready for the next step. But would he know what to do? He? They? She didn't care. The smell, the music, and the darkness combined to enhance one another. And the pain on her nipples pushed her ever higher.

She felt fingers opening her and something slowly penetrating her pussy. A dildo. Large. Filling. Pressing and opening. She wanted to resist. It was almost too big. It wouldn't. . . . Yet it did. Then it withdrew, and penetrated again.

Then a hand landed on one of her ass cheeks. The spank was more noise than substance, and the sound was muffled by the music from the earphones. More slaps. No rhythm. Long pauses, then two or three quick slaps. And the constant movement of the dildo. And the pulling on her nipples. Ever higher. Ever higher.

The men seemed to know exactly how to drive her higher, yet not let her near climax. How long? Minutes? Hours? Her cheeks became hot and supersensitive. Like the clips, the slaps were painful, yet not quite painful. It was pure pleasure. She had never liked serious pain, although she and Henry had gotten pretty deeply into this kind of play. Now it was just the right mix, the perfect spice.

Suddenly hands parted her cheeks and something slippery and cold was being spread on her anus. "No," she said. "Don't." Spaceship. That was the word she could use if she really wanted everything to end. Did she? "No," she said again.

Yes. It was happening. With the dildo now still in her pussy, filling her totally, something slender and cold was being pushed into her rear hole. Henry had tried anal sex once or twice, but she had never really been comfortable with it. Now, slowly being penetrated by a slim anal dildo, she felt opened as she had never been before. Her hips bucked, seemingly of their own volition. She thrashed her limbs to the extent allowed by her restraints. She arched her back, and her moans became deafening, even over the music in her ears.

"God," she shrieked, and the dildo sunk deeper into her rear passage. "Oh God." She could no more control her climax than she could control the objects invading her body. She came, unable to do anything but ride the tide of pleasure, ride it out long and hard, like a surfer riding a powerful wave farther and farther, hoping it would never reach the shore. Yet it did. Occasionally in her lovemaking, she could rise to more than one orgasm, but now she was so completely satiated that her body was capable of nothing more.

As she lay, totally spent, the objects were removed from her body and her wrists and ankles were unfastened from the legs of the bench. She lay, still blindfolded, for several minutes, then slowly roused herself and walked toward the shower she knew lay beyond the door. She would take a long hot shower and go home, knowing she would be back many more times.

In another area of the house, Maria sat, surrounded by four small creatures with scaly, bluish skin and overly large heads and eyes. The one who called himself Joe smiled. "That was the best yet," he said. "Her orgasm will fuel our ship for many miles of travel."

Maria marveled at their ability to harness such energy and transfer it to their marooned ship. "Do you need much more?" she asked, worried that they would soon be gone. Their business was thriving, and no woman had ever failed to return.

He smiled softly, his strange features becoming almost handsome, for an alien. "We still need more energy, and we do so enjoy the way we get it. The thrill of feeling a climax like we do is as good as the actual orgasm."

Maria grinned back. "Well, we've got time before Nancy Stern gets here. How about coming up to my bedroom and I'll give you enough energy to travel to the moon? And back."

The Corset

I WAS STANDING in front of a rack of Victorian corsets in my favorite sex shop, my cock flaccid, my mind wandering. I have several regular play partners, and I keep lots of luscious outfits for them, but I'm always on the lookout for new, exciting bits of erotic lingerie that I can share with my pets.

Yes, pets. Plural. I know it's not fashionable in this day and age to date more than one woman at a time, but I'm not ready to settle down to one flavor yet. Every one of my partners knows that she is not my one and only, and each is free to date anyone else she chooses. I always take care to use a condom, two if I want to play the back way, if you catch my drift, and I am sure to have myself tested for any nasty little germs at least four times a year. That's the way I choose to live, and, if others want to share my lifestyle, that's great. If not, that's fine, too.

Anyway, I was standing, fingering a particularly lovely satin corset, when a slightly shy-looking young woman walked into the shop. She looked around, obviously nervous about her first visit to a sex shop, then almost tiptoed toward the rack behind which I was standing. As she walked, I watched. She was a moderately pretty young woman, in her early twenties, I'd guess, with soft brown hair curling to her shoulders, large blue eyes, and a small, tight body. In her jeans and tank top, she looked like she was in good shape, but not overly muscled.

She saw me, looked at me for a moment, then turned away, blushing. Now I'm not at all bad to look at—tall, with black hair, deep brown eyes, and a body my pets call hunky. I smile at one woman's term for me. She refers to me as a major babe. As someone who prides himself on being very male, being a babe isn't my idea of a compliment, but she means it as such so I assume that women like what they see.

I think the young woman beside me did, too. "Good afternoon," I said softly. "I'm Clint."

When she remained silent, I said, "It's really okay to talk to strangers. My mother always said you never meet anyone truly exciting unless you occasionally take a chance."

I heard her soft chuckle. "I'm Gwen."

"Your first time here?" I asked.

"I used to come here a lot, but it's been a long time. I'm just looking."

Never one for much subtlety, I asked, "Did your boyfriend send you out to buy something special?"

"Oh no. We broke up two months ago. It was really bad. I guess that I'm just trying to feel feminine again." She didn't realize that she was stroking the smooth fabric of a tightly boned, midnight blue silk corset.

"I'm sorry that you two broke up, but it's probably for the best. I don't think he understood you."

"Excuse me?" Without realizing it, she continued to run her fingers over the stays, rigid and constricting.

"I think you want to feel something like that corset you're caressing on your body, the laces being drawn tighter and tighter."

She dropped her hand as if the corset had suddenly grown tentacles. "I beg your pardon?"

"That's a restraining garment. It gives the wearer the feeling of being tightly bound." I lifted the hanger from the rack and showed Gwen several small loops of fabric. "There are also places for bindings to be attached."

Gwen stared as I slowly inserted one finger into a loop, then withdrew it. Slowly, in and out, my finger fucked the loop. Her eyes never left my hand. I took an educated guess. "Your boyfriend didn't understand your needs, did he? Maybe he was pretty straight?"

"Very," she whispered.

"So why don't you try this on? There's a fitting room in the back."

"I'm sorry," she said, her voice trembling. "I think you have the wrong idea."

"I'm seldom wrong. I understand your hesitation, but it's really silly to deny something so obvious, and something that could give us both so much pleasure. I'd love to see you in that. Close your eyes and think about yourself in that corset, with me beside you. Give yourself the opportunity to have some fun and remember how good it used to be before your boyfriend loused it all up."

"But it's kinky."

Without overly pressuring her, I said, "And what's wrong with kinky, if it gives pleasure? Please."

She looked from the garment to my face, then back again.

"You'll be in a public place, and nothing can happen that you don't want. The clerk's an old friend of mine, and he will leave us alone. But if you call out, he'll be on me real quick. He won't jeopardize a customer, ever. I'm in here a lot, and I would endanger his friendly attitude if I got the least bit out of line." I paused, then whispered, "Please."

Without another word she nodded, took the corset from my hand, and walked toward the curtained-off rear of the store. I waited several minutes, then made eye contact with Brandon, the store's owner and clerk. He nodded, and I walked into the back.

In the corner of the storage area there was a large

area separated from the rest of the room by heavy drapes. "Gwen?" I whispered.

"Yes," I heard from behind the drapes.

"May I see how that looks?" I wanted her full agreement.

"I can't get it fastened," she said. "I guess I could use some help."

I slipped through the drapes and just gazed at her. She had removed all her clothes and was almost wearing the blue corset. It had a line of hooks up the back, and she had closed only the bottom half. "Here," I said, "let me help you." I pulled the corset and fastened the remaining hooks, then looked into her eyes in the full-length mirror that covered two walls. "It's not nearly tight enough. Shall I show you?"

She stared at me, then nodded.

The laces were in the front so I moved between her and the mirror, then crouched and took the ends of the laces and wound them around my hands. I pulled. Hard, slowly, smoothly until I knew her waist was being tightly compressed. I moved so we could both see her. The sight was maximally erotic. The deep blue covered her from hips to breasts, with long blue garters dangling below. I could just make out her soft brown pubic hair. "More?" I whispered.

"Yes," she said. I pulled the laces tighter, and she gasped.

"Let me make this better," I said. I knew this garment well since I had several versions for my friends to wear, so I reached beneath Gwen's breasts and deftly removed the fabric that covered them.

"Oh," she said as two pieces of fabric came away in my hands. Now the corset pulled her ribs and waist tightly but fully revealed her small tight breasts.

"God, you're gorgeous in that." I whispered in her ear. "I want to show you more."

I could tell from her face that she was lost in an erotic fog. She couldn't speak, so I slipped out of the dressing room and returned quickly with other items from the store. I pulled a special pair of long black gloves onto her arms and clipped small hooks to the loops on the sides of the corset, effectively imprisoning her elbows against her sides. Her nipples were hard little buttons reaching forward. "Look at yourself," I said. "You're so beautiful, and so hot." I walked behind her and cupped her breasts. Then I pinched her nipples hard. "And you love it. Tell me how you love this."

"Oh God," she moaned.

"This is the real you. You've been trying to deny it, but it just won't work. You need it."

"Yes," she groaned. "I need this so much."

I reached down and unzipped the front of my jeans, allowing my now rigid cock to spring free. "Show me how much."

Without hesitation, Gwen knelt and took my hard

member into her soft mouth. "Slowly," I told her. "There's no hurry."

She sat back on her haunches and said, "Yes, there is. I want you."

I laughed. "Then you shall have me." There was a small straight chair in the corner of the room. I unfastened her elbows from the sides of the corset and fastened them together. Then I bent her forward and placed her hands on the seat of the chair. Her ass cheeks were beautiful with wisps of pussy hair visible. I quickly sheathed my cock in latex, then parted her cheeks. Unerringly, my erection found her pussy hole and I plunged inside. At the same time I reached around and roughly squeezed one breast with one hand. I found her clit with the other.

It took only a moment until she screamed and I felt the spasms of her pussy on my cock. That was all my heated flesh needed, and I came with a roar. After a few moments, I released her elbows and handed her my handkerchief so she could clean up her juices. I removed the condom and rezipped my pants. "I think you've learned about yourself today."

"Oh yes," she said, grinning. "It's foolish of me to pretend. I can't settle for less than what I need."

"I would like to get to know you better," I said. It had been so quick that I wanted time to savor her. "Just for fun and games, and anything else we can find."

"I think I'd like that. Maybe this time we could talk a bit before—"

I laughed. "You know, I think this is the beginning of something rather special."

"I hope so," she said. "How about we get some coffee?" She hesitated, looking down at the corset. "And get me out of this thing. . . . For the moment."

The Gloves

*I*T MUST HAVE BEEN the gloves. I remember that night clearly, and it was the gloves. And the Bloody Marys.

Larry and I had been invited to a formal thing at his boss's country club, and I decided to wear a black strapless number that I had worn a few times before. To give it new life, I found a long, cream-colored silk scarf in a department store. I draped it around my neck and allowed the ends to trail down my back. I also found a pair of long, cream-colored satin gloves that came up well past my elbows to wear with the outfit. If I do say so myself, I looked smashing.

At the party, I felt different, somehow, sensuous and powerful. During the evening, we had a sumptuous meal, and I drank quite a few of those wonderfully spicy tomato juice concoctions. After dinner I danced with

Larry's boss, and with several of his coworkers. All of them commented on how sexy I looked. I also danced with Larry several times, and he held me close and nibbled on my ear. It was fantastic.

We had hired a limo for the evening, knowing that we would probably drink a bit too much, so when we were ready to leave, there it was, waiting in front of the club, a uniformed chauffeur in the driver's seat. Giggling and knowing that we had the use of the limo for another hour, I said, "Let's drive around for a while." Then I leaned over and whispered to Larry, "Let's give the driver a bit of a show."

Now let me tell you that Larry is always willing for me to show off my body to men. He loves it when I wear a skimpy bikini and, on occasion, when I'm wearing a tight skirt, he's been known to have me remove my panties and spread my legs for anyone who might be watching. Tonight, he seemed willing to play.

"Hey, driver," he said, "drive north on the highway until you get to the state line, then turn around and drive back again." In a stage whisper he said, "That should take about an hour." Then he started kissing me—deep, tongue-dueling kisses that weakened my knees and moistened my pussy. "Are you getting hot?" he asked.

"Yes," I said, moving my hips to try to relieve the ache in my cunt.

"Then let's show the driver what he's missing."

Deftly, Larry grabbed the zipper tab at the back of my dress and pulled it all the way down, allowing the top to fall to my waist. I was wearing my black strapless bustier that cinched my waist and lifted my ample tits. I watched as the driver moved his rearview mirror so he had a good view of the carryings-on in his backseat.

"He's watching," I said, rubbing my still-gloved hands over the silky fabric of the cincher.

"Oh yes," Larry said. "He's getting a good view. Show him those gorgeous tits."

I still had my gloves on, and my satin-covered hands against my skin made it feel as if someone else was touching my body, but touching it exactly where and how I wanted to be touched. I lifted my right breast out of the cup and held it for Larry to lick. "Yes, baby," I said as his head dipped toward my aching nipple. "Suck and lick it." I cupped the back of Larry's head with my gloved hand and massaged his neck as he suckled. With his face against my chest, I was able to make eye contact with the driver as he glanced in the mirror.

I rubbed my satiny fingers over Larry's cheeks as he nursed on my flesh. I unbuttoned his shirt and pulled it open, rubbing my hands over his smooth, hairless chest. My hands were everywhere. It was as if they had a mind of their own. I unzipped Larry's pants and pulled out his hard cock, stroking it, feeling it harden and swell.

"Ma'am," the driver suddenly said softly, his voice trembling a bit. "If you're going to keep doing things like that, I'd better pull over. I can't drive and watch, and I can't stop watching. I don't want us to end up in the hospital."

I put my hand beneath Larry's chin and lifted his face. "Let's have him pull over and watch," I said. "Is that okay with you?" I trusted that Larry wouldn't agree if something made him uncomfortable. He grinned, then whispered, "I am even willing to share if you want to."

Did I want to? I had always had fantasies about two men pleasuring me at the same time, but I never dreamed it might come true. But here I was, half-naked, wearing those incredibly sexy long gloves, Larry's cock in my hand, and a nice-looking man about to join us. "Pull over," I said, "in some private spot."

"I know this area. There's an old golf course just off this exit. I can park there where no one will see."

He quickly exited the highway, and soon we were parked in a darkened lot. "Now," I said, "if you really want to watch, why don't you come back here and see everything up close—" I giggled "—and personal, as they say on TV."

Quickly the driver flicked off the lights, tuned the radio to a soft music station, and moved into the back-seat. "It's very dark," Larry said as the driver settled himself on the side opposite to where Larry was sitting. Two hot, hungry men, one on each side of me. I was in heaven.

The driver turned on one of those goose-neck reading lights found in some limos and moved the light so the bright, warm beam illuminated my swollen breast. I quickly freed the other one from my bustier. "What's your name?" I asked the driver.

"Chet," he said, his eyes glued to my hardened nipple.

"Want to play, Chet?" I asked, stroking his cheek with my gloved hand.

Silently, he raised his eyes and looked into mine. I cupped my right breast and offered it to my husband, who immediately started to nip at the tight nub. I cupped my left breast and looked at Chet. As if offered a feast, he bowed his head and took the nipple into his hot mouth. I leaned back on the leather seat, stroking the necks of two men as their mouths played havoc with senses. Two mouths. Two sets of teeth. Two tongues. It was my fantasy, only better than I could have imagined. I closed my eyes and felt heat flow from my tits to my wide-open pussy.

The dress was split up the side so, as I allowed my legs to part, my thighs were exposed. Larry lifted his head. "She's got gorgeous legs," he said to Chet. "And they're so soft. Feel."

Larry slid his fingertips up the inside of my right thigh above my stockings, and, with little coaxing, Chet's hand began to stroke my left. I felt Chet's confidence in the whole situation grow, and his hand become bolder as he brushed the crotch of my soaked panties. As Chet's fingers began to work magic between my legs, Larry pinched my nipples.

"Oh God," I hissed.

"Yes, baby," Larry purred. "I'm pinching your tits while a strange man is stroking your pussy. It makes you so hot, doesn't it?"

"Yes," I moaned, unable to think clearly anymore. My body was on fire, my pussy lips swollen and open, my cunt aching to be filled.

"Help me," Larry said to Chet. Together they lifted my ass and pulled off my panties. I stretched my legs out in the long body of the limo, my ankles wide apart. "Do you want to do her?" Larry asked Chet. "Not with your cock. I'll always keep that for myself, but with your hands and your mouth?"

Chet slid off the seat and crouched between my spread legs. "God, you've got a hot box, lady," he groaned, his mouth finding my clit, his fingers entering my pussy.

"Yes, yes, yes," I said. It was almost more than I could take. Larry kept pinching my nipples, just this side of severe pain, while Chet's mouth sucked and his tongue flicked and his fingers filled me. I came. I wanted to hold back, make it last, but I couldn't. I came hard and fast and long. Wave after wave of liquid heat washed over me, and I screamed.

The two men kept up the sensations until I literally

had to tell them to stop. There was a bottle of champagne in a cooler tucked into a compartment under the seat, and Chet opened it. In silence, we drank some straight from the bottle.

After I had had a few minutes to calm down, I looked at Larry and took his hard cock in my still-gloved hand. He smiled as I turned and, with my other hand, unzipped Chet's fly and pulled out his immense cock. As I held each cock, I felt their weight. My husband's was shorter, but thicker, while Chet's was long and slender, with a dark purple head.

I slid my slippery hands all over the two cocks. "That's dynamite," Larry said, panting. "Those gloves make it feel totally different."

"I just know you feel so good, ma'am," Chet said. "But I'm afraid if you keep doing that I'm going to mess up your clothes."

"She has others," Larry said. I turned and saw that his eyes were riveted on Chet's cock in my hand. "Do it," he moaned. "Make him come."

I caressed and rubbed, then slid my hand into his pants and cupped his balls. "Lady," he groaned.

Larry pulled at one of my gloves until it came off, wrapped it around his cock and rubbed the length of his erect shaft. "Do him," he said.

I used my ungloved hand to tickle Chet's balls while my gloved one continued its relentless manipulation of his cock.

"I'm gonna come if you keep that up," he moaned.

"I hope so," I said. "Come for me, baby. Let me watch you spurt all over. Show me. Let me watch you both come." This was heaven. Two men, stretched out in the back of the limo, cocks hard and hungry, Larry rubbing his with my glove, Chet moaning as I jerked him off. Breathing was heavy, bodies trembled, and, almost simultaneously, the two cocks erupted, spurts of thick white jism arching onto the floor of the limo.

A while later, we rezipped and rearranged. Wordlessly, Chet got out and returned to the driver's seat. We drove home in silence, Larry's arms around me. When we arrived at our house, Larry signed the charge slip and added a healthy tip for our partner in sex. "I have your number," Larry said. "I think you can be sure we'll be calling on your—" he paused "—services again."

"I certainly hope so," Chet said as he slowly pulled away.

Family Jewels

ONE EVENING

BRAD AND I have been married for almost three years, and I'm still amazed by how sexy he is. Like Superman, beneath his mild-mannered exterior beats the heart of a hot, hungry sex maniac, and I'm beginning to think he's turned me into a fiend as well. We make love almost every night, and we have both become very creative at teasing and game playing.

One Saturday afternoon about a month ago, I was cleaning out an old closet, and I found the hand-decorated shoe box I used to keep all my junk jewelry in during high school. It had been five years since I had last rummaged in my treasures, so I sat on the hall floor and removed the lid from the box. With a wistful smile, I grabbed a handful of beaded necklaces.

I leaned against the wall and recalled the afternoons I spent with friends wandering through the local discount store, stocking up on plastic jewelry. During my senior year in high school, I even got a job in the cosmetics department, not only for the salary but also for the ten percent discount I got.

Sighing with pleasure at the memory, I filled my fingers with earrings, bracelets, and necklaces in a rainbow of colors, gold and silver. Many of the pieces were encrusted with rhinestones and chips of colored glass, and several of the gaudy rings had huge stones and fake pearls. Buried at the bottom were a few neck chains on which I used to hang charm holders and pendants engraved with my name or initials and tiny replicas of animals, shoes, or hearts.

As I picked up a pair of long, dangly golden earrings, I started thinking. I smiled and began rushing around the house. I knew I had to hurry if I was going to be ready by the time Brad got home from doing his errands.

In the back of one of my bureau drawers I found several large silky scarves. After stripping off all my clothes, I wrapped one around my ample breasts and put aside another to cover the lower half of my face. I snapped two golden chains together and fastened them around my waist, then draped one large scarf over the waist chain in the front and another in the back. I put on a pair of dangly golden earrings, pinned an ornate necklace into the top of my long brown hair so it hung over my forehead, and covered my arms with harem-style bracelets. I hung three heavy beaded necklaces around my neck, fastened several bracelets around my ankles, and put a ring on each finger. To complete the outfit, I added bright red lipstick and heavy, dark green eyeshadow. As I heard Brad slam the front door I bobby-pinned the scarf in place over the lower half of my face.

"Sandy!" Brad yelled, "I'm home."

"In here," I answered. "In the bedroom." I struck a seductive pose and waited. Brad walked into the room, and I watched his eyes roam over my body. I could see what he saw reflected in the mirror behind him. My nipples were hard and showed clearly through the scarf that tried unsuccessfully to hold them. My dark, fluffy pubic hair made a slight bulge in the front of the scarf that hung between my knees. As I looked at my husband and slowly moved my hips, I saw a matching bulge appear in the front of Brad's jeans.

"Sit down and don't move a muscle," I said, my breath making the face scarf flutter against my lips. "You're in for a show." I pushed Brad down onto the foot of the bed, turned on the radio, and turned it to an easy-listening station.

I picked up the beat of a soft-rock song and began to dance around the room, watching Brad's eyes follow my every move. I pinched my nipples through the silky fabric and then slid my palms over their pebbled tips.

"Oh, Sandy," Brad said. "You make me so hot." I

watched him shift position to make more room for his cock inside his tight jeans.

"Poor darling," I breathed. I danced over to him and unzipped his pants. He tried to reach out for me, but I whispered, "I told you not to move." I fumbled with his underwear and pulled out his hard, throbbing cock. "I just want to give him some air," I said, slipping the tip under my face scarf and planting a lipsticked kiss on the end. Then I blew a stream of cool air over his exposed erection. "That should help."

Slowly, I reached behind my back and untied the scarf that covered my breasts. Holding the multicolored fabric against my nipples, I rubbed back and forth against it, arching my back like a cat in heat.

I slowly slid the wisp of fabric across his face, then kissed his mouth through the two layers of silk. "Filter-tip kissing," I whispered. "That's all for now." I dropped the scarf that had tied my tits onto the bed.

Now that my breasts were freed from their confinement, I wriggled my shoulders so that they swayed and bounced before Brad's hungry eyes. As my hips undulated, I reached around and grasped the end of the scarf that hung from my waist in back. I brushed the silken fabric over the end of Brad's huge cock, then again kissed the tip of his organ through the material. "Not unfiltered just yet," I said, my breath heavy and hot against the silk. I slid my hand up and down his covered shaft until I could see a small drop of pre-come form. Then I handed the end of the scarf to him. "Just hold that, baby," I told him, then slowly backed away until the scarf slid from the waist chain.

Knowing that my firm ass was now bare, I turned and shimmied, then grabbed my cheeks and pulled them apart, giving my husband a good view of my puckered hole.

"Oh, honey," Brad moaned, "you're killing me." I knew that he was thinking about ass fucking, one of his favorite pleasures. He was suffering the delicious torment of being teased and loving every moment of it.

With my back still facing Brad, I took the end of the scarf that covered my pussy in the front, and handed it to him between my legs. "Now you get to play," I said to him. He knew exactly what I wanted. What we both wanted.

"I love playing with you," Brad said, sliding the end of the scarf up the insides of my thighs. "So stand still, baby, and let me play." He raised his hand, lifting his end of the scarf, pressing the material against my wet pussy. Then, as he slowly pulled the scarf from the waist chain, it slid between my swollen lips and rubbed against my hard clit.

"Getting hot, too, darling?" Brad asked.

"Oh yes," I whispered as I turned around. "But today it's my party. Lie back."

As he lay back on the bed I admired the exaggerated contrast between us. He lay there, still fully dressed, with his cock standing at full attention and sticking through the fly of his jeans. I was naked, with a scarf over my face and dozens of pieces of jewelry adorning my body. I loved it just this way. As Brad started to unbutton his shirt, the scarves gave me an idea.

"Don't," I said. His hands froze, and he watched me pick up one of the lengths of silk. "Now, give me your wrist." Brad held out his right arm, his eyes gleaming. I looped the end of one scarf around his wrist, quickly tying it to one side of the bed frame. We'd tried light bondage for the first time about a month earlier, and it had led to a wild night of uninhibited fucking. To make sure everything was okay now, I looked into Brad's eyes. I smiled at the unrestrained lust I saw, then walked to the other side of the bed and quickly tied his other wrist.

"Now, baby," I purred, "let's see how much you want me." I leaned over and tickled the end of his exposed cock with one long earring. I watched as another drop of fluid oozed out. "Oh yes, that's good. I want you to want me very much." I climbed onto the bed and, with one knee on either side of his chest, dangled one breast above his open mouth.

"Want to suck me?" I asked.

"Oh baby," he whispered, his breathing so heavy that he was barely able to get the words out.

I let my engorged nipple brush his lips, then I filled his mouth with my flesh. "Suck it good, honey," I said. "Suck it good." His mouth tugged rhythmically at my sensitive nipple and made my pussy quiver and twitch. I had to have him, yet I wanted to continue to tease. Without pulling my tit from his mouth, I lowered my body until my wet labia touched the end of his cock. I reached between my legs, wrapped my hand around his throbbing erection, and rubbed it against my clit.

"Baby," Brad said, my tit slipping from his mouth, "let me fuck you."

"You suck, I'll do the fucking." I put my other nipple in his mouth, and he resumed almost nursing at my breast. I continued rubbing his cock against my clit until I thought I would explode from the pleasure of it, then I placed Brad's purple cock head at the opening of my sopping cunt, then, inch by slow inch, I allowed my body to drop. Gradually his pole filled me. I could feel his muscles tense as he pulled at the scarves holding his arms. He wanted to control our fucking, but he quickly realized that since he couldn't use his arms, I was in charge.

Suddenly his hips bucked, trying to take me more quickly than I wanted. I pulled back and glared at him. "Bad boy," I said. "This is my party."

His eyes glowed hungrily, but he smiled at me. "I want your hot and wet pussy surrounding my cock. Please," he said.

"I like that," I said. "Ask nice."

"Please, baby. Let me fill you up."

I leaned back and slowly lowered my pussy onto his shaft. Then I held completely still and felt his cock twitch and wiggle deep inside of me. "Like that?" I asked sweetly, knowing he wanted much more.

He hesitated. I knew he wanted me to move and fuck his cock, but he said, "Whatever you want, baby."

"Well right now, I want you bad." I raised my body, then dropped onto his cock. Quickly, I established a rhythm, raising my hips, then impaling myself on his prick. Over and over I fucked him, until I knew I was almost there. I reached down and fingered my clit, then exploded as his cock spurted deep inside my hot pussy. My hips bucked against Brad's as we both screamed our climax.

I quickly untied Brad's wrists, and we lay together. "You know, baby," Brad said, "that was terrific. But I'll get back at you for teasing me."

I knew he would, and I looked forward to it. But I never dreamed that my jewelry would give him the means.

Family Jewels

A FEW DAYS LATER

A FEW DAYS LATER, I arrived home from work to find that Brad had picked up our favorite Indian food from a local restaurant. To go with the spicy-hot food, we consumed several bottles of cold beer. After dinner, Brad said, "I liked the way you looked naked, in all that jewelry the other night. Would you dress up for me like that again tonight?"

After we cleaned up the dinner remains, we went into the bedroom. "I want you naked," he said, and I willingly obliged. Then he took out the shoe box and handed me necklaces, earrings, and bracelets for both my wrists and ankles. He even gave me a waist chain, which I put around my middle. "Like this?" I asked.

"You look wonderful. Now lie down."

From the gleam in his eye, I knew he had something devilish in mind, and I was eager to know what it was. Sensuously, I stretched out on the bed, naked except for my adornments.

Brad picked up a small safety pin from the bed table. "Now, to continue." He took the pin and, carefully so I didn't get stuck, slid it through one of my bracelets and used it to pin my wrist to the sheet so my arm was straight out at shoulder level. Quickly, he similarly pinned my other wrist.

"Those bracelets are very flimsy," Brad purred, "and you could pull free at any time if—" he hesitated "—you wanted to break them. But they're very valuable, and you wouldn't want them broken, would you?"

"Oh no," I whispered, playing the game that my dime-store jewelry was somehow worth millions. It was strange and highly exciting, lying here, naked, covered with jewelry, while Brad was still fully dressed.

"I think you need more jewelry," he said, taking a strand of orange beads from the box. He opened the clasp and wrapped the necklace around my upper thigh so the cool beads just brushed my pussy hair. Then he slipped the necklace through the waist chain and fastened the clasp. "Now, you wouldn't want to break any of these, so don't move suddenly," he said, a leering smile on his face. He quickly wrapped a purple strand around my other thigh and slid it through the waist chain as well. It was a strange feeling, like being chained up. And it was almost as though the beads were pulling my pussy lips apart. I was breathless, my body quivering from the hunger that was flowing through my veins.

"Good," Brad purred. "Very good." He surveyed my body. "Now for your ankles." He looped a string of hot pink beads through an ankle bracelet on one leg and a navy blue one through a chain on the other. Then he drew both necklaces up through the waist chain, forcing my legs to bend at the knees. The only way to get my legs comfortable was to let them fall open so that my soaked pussy was exposed, framed in colored beads.

"Oh, I like the way that looks," Brad said. "I bought a few necklaces of my own today," he said, "and I cut open the strings." He chuckled. "Of course, I didn't want to destroy the valuable ones." I smiled at his joke. Then Brad showed me a bowl filled with loose, colored plastic beads, and he ran his fingers through his hoard.

He dug into the bowl, took a handful of beads, and held them over my breasts. Slowly, he let them pour through his spread fingers and fall soft and cool on my heated flesh. Gently, he again filled his hands with beads and used them to caress and massage my globes, ribs, and belly. He covered my body with the round pieces of plastic and rolled them everywhere.

"I want you to know that I've washed all of these thoroughly." I didn't have long to wonder why he'd said that. He held a string of pearly white beads, slid them down my belly, and dangled them against my pussy hair.

"There's one place you don't have jewels yet," he said, then knelt between my spread knees. One bead at a time, he inserted the entire strand of pearls into my soaking cunt. The feeling was so erotic that it was hard not to come right then.

"Now, I can't leave them in there too long," he said, "or they might be damaged." He leaned over, his mouth close to my swollen lips. "Let me see if I can find them."

He looked for the beads, all right, with his mouth. He slowly explored every fold of my cunt, murmuring occasionally, "Not here." He slid his lips over my hard clit. "Not here either." Then his tongue found the small loop of beads that he had left protruding from my pussy. "There they are," he purred, his breath hot on my wet skin.

I felt him catch the loop with his tongue and grasp it with his teeth. Bead by bead he pulled the pearls out of my pussy. "I'm going to come," I screamed.

"Not just yet, baby." Leaving the pearls still partly inside of me, Brad quickly pulled off his clothes. I could tell by his straining cock that this torture was as exciting for him as it was for me. "I want to try one more thing before I fuck you," he said. He picked up all the loose beads and refilled the bowl. Then he knelt over the bowl and plunged his cock into the beads. "I knew it would feel sensational," he said, withdrawing and inserting his cock over and over again. I watched him fuck the bowl of plastic beads, one or two beads sticking to the wet, sticky end of his big, hard rod. "They feel so cool as they slide over my hot prick."

It was almost torture watching him as he fucked the bowl of beads for a full minute. I wanted his cock inside of me, and I could tell he was getting very close. "Save that for me," I said.

"Don't worry, baby," Brad said, showing me his eager cock. "This is all for you."

He crouched between my spread knees and rubbed the exposed loop of pearls over my cunt, paying special attention to my hardened clit. I was so hot I yelled, "Fuck me now."

"Bad girl," he said, smiling. "This is my party now." He leaned down and took the bead loop with his teeth and again began to pull the rest of the strand from my pussy. When the last bead finally popped from my body, he leaned over and teased me with his prick. Then, inch by inch he inserted his cock into me.

I was beyond caring about my "valuable jewelry." I pulled on the necklaces holding my ankles and quickly broke them both. I wrapped my legs around Brad's waist and drove him hard into my body, enjoying the odd pressure of the beads that surrounded my upper thighs. As I pulled him hard inside of me a second time, I came. Brad came only moments later.

Later, lying next to each other, our breathing slowly returned to normal. "Well, baby," Brad said, holding up the two broken necklaces, "you've broken two pieces of the family jewels."

I grabbed his now flaccid cock. "The family jewels are just fine. But we'll have to go to the store and buy some more plastic beads. I want a rematch."

"So do I, baby. So do I."

In the Shower

H E'S GOING to be home in just a few hours, Jenny thought as she opened the apartment door and dumped the groceries on the kitchen table. Steak, baked potatoes, salad, and asparagus. She arranged the ingredients for a good, home-cooked meal on the counter. And, she thought, grinning, me for dessert.

Jenny's husband, Karl, had been away for almost three weeks on a business trip and, having wrapped up a big sale, was due home on a flight landing at five-thirty. She checked to see whether the flight was landing on time and was glad that everything was on schedule. "Let's see," Jenny mumbled, "landing at five-thirty, an hour to get his luggage and clear customs, and half an hour from the airport to here. Seven. So I'll plan dinner for seven-thirty, but I won't put the steak on until he's home."

She looked again at her watch. Five-forty. He should be pulling up to the gate. I've got time for a quick shower, and then I'll get organized. Leaving all the groceries on the counter, Jenny walked into the bedroom and stripped off her work clothes. Dressed in only her bra and panties, she walked into the bathroom and adjusted the shower until the temperature was just right. She quickly pulled off her underwear and stepped beneath the pounding water. With a long sigh, she let the water beat on the back of her neck. With her back to the shower curtain, she began to soap her body.

Suddenly she heard a sound behind her and felt cool air on her wet back. "Guess who?"

"Karl, baby," she said, placing her hand over her pounding heart. "You startled the hell out of me." She turned and saw that her husband of four years was naked and had stepped into the shower. "I didn't expect you until about seven," she said, calming her breathing.

"I couldn't wait to get home, so I managed to catch an earlier flight. I wanted to call, but I just had no time. I dashed and just made it as the doors were closing. Sorry I'm early?"

"Oh, baby, not at all." She wrapped her arms around her husband and held him against her wet, naked body. Her mouth found his, and they kissed as the water pounded around them. As they parted, she said, "I missed you so much."

Karl grabbed her hand and put it on his swollen

cock. "I missed you, too." He took the bar of soap and rubbed it in his hands. When he was all lathery, he said, "You wanted to wash before I got home, and I wouldn't want to stop you." He held her against him and used his soapy hands to rub her back. He kneaded her muscles and rubbed up and down the length of her spine. Adding more lather, he cupped her ass cheeks and pulled them apart as he also pressed her mound against his hard cock.

"Umm," she purred, "that feels so good."

"It sure does. Now turn around." As Jenny turned, Karl again lathered his hands. She pressed her back against his chest and wiggled her soapy butt against his crotch. His palms found her breasts, and his slippery hands lifted her heavy tits and rubbed the nipples. He rolled first one hardening bud then the other between his fingers.

Jenny felt her knees almost give way beneath the sensual onslaught. His hands were everywhere, slick and slippery, massaging and inflaming. Again and again he relathered his hands and found new places to rub. He knelt on the shower floor and rubbed her legs and feet, then ran his hands up the insides of her thighs.

"I've got to get you all clean," Karl said, rinsing his fingers, then sliding them between her legs, rubbing the places now slippery with her juices. "All over."

Playfully, Jenny pushed his hands away and then

soaped hers. "You know," she said, her breathing ragged, "you've been flying for several hours, probably got all dirty and sweaty." She pulled him back to a standing position and rubbed his hairy chest. "Two can play this game."

She rubbed and caressed Karl's body with slippery hands, adding more soap from time to time. She stroked his back, his buttocks, his legs, his arms, and his neck, avoiding his cock and balls. With an impish grin, she said, "I'm sure you need to get clean all over."

Hot water cascading over her head, she lathered her hands and knelt on the bathtub floor. Carefully insinuating her fingers in every crevice, she soaped his balls, then his fully erect cock. As she washed him, she thought about oral sex. She knew that Karl wanted her to suck him, but every time she had thought about it in the past, it had made her gag. Now, however, with his cock at eye level, all soapy and clean, she thought she might be able to do it, or at least lick him, and what better welcome home gift for him.

She turned him so the water flowed over his belly and cock, then, when he was all rinsed, turned him again until his back was to the water. Then she said, "You know, eventually I have to dry you off. Why not start now?" She licked the length of his cock, tasting the clean water that covered him. As she licked, she cupped his testicles in her hand. "Umm," she purred. "You really taste good."

Jenny felt Karl's body tense as she again ran her tongue the length of the underside of his erection. "Oh God," he moaned. "You don't have to do that, you know."

"I know."

"Baby, it feels so good."

"I know that, too." A small bit of fluid flowed from the tip of her husband's prick, so Jenny tentatively touched her tongue to it. Tangy and salty, she thought, but not unpleasant. She pressed the flat of her tongue against the tip of his cock and licked. Not unpleasant at all. Could she go further? she wondered. Could she actually suck it into her mouth? Well, she thought, nothing ventured.

She formed her lips into an O and pressed her mouth to the head of Karl's throbbing member. The head popped into her mouth, then she drew back and it pulled out again. She did this several times, until she felt Karl lean back. "Baby," he said, "that's the most wonderful thing you could do, but you better stop before you get a mouthful of me."

I don't think I'm ready for that, she thought, but this isn't nearly as bad as I had expected. Karl grabbed her by her armpits and pulled her up, then knelt down and put his mouth against her pubic mound, finding her clit with his tongue. The sensations were electric, and Jenny was quickly aroused to the point of near-orgasm. Obviously knowing her arousal level, Karl stood and pressed her back against the wall of the shower. As the water poured over them, he lifted one of her legs, supporting her weight with his large body. Then he drove his cock into her waiting pussy.

He thrust again and again, driving her higher, pressing her back against the wall. "Yes, baby," he moaned. "Oh yes."

She dug her fingernails into his ass cheeks, pulling him still closer. With matching screams, the two climaxed almost simultaneously.

Panting and almost unable to stand, the two quickly rinsed off any lingering soap, climbed out of the shower, and, wrapped in fluffy towels, collapsed onto the bed. "Oh baby," Karl moaned. "That was sensational. I never expected you to do that."

"Me neither," Jenny said, her pulse slowly returning to normal, "but it just seemed right. Was what I did okay?"

Karl's chuckle was deep and warm. He pulled her close. "It was wonderful, baby. And any time you want to do it again, in or out of the shower, I'm willing. Eager. But if you don't, that's fine, too."

"Yeah," she said. "I know that. That's why I could do it, and it was really okay."

"You're fantastic." Just then his stomach rumbled. "You're also a great cook, you know."

Jenny giggled. "Okay. I get the hint."

"And after dinner," Karl said, "I want you for dessert."

"Exactly what I had in mind."

The Mile-High Club

*I*T HAD BEEN a long period of frustration for my husband, Mark, and me. Together we owned and operated Littleton's Imports, and we had been traveling through the Far East on a buying trip for almost twelve days. We had had almost no privacy and had spent most of our time so tired that we had little desire for each other anyway. With no one in the third of the three-across seats, we'd managed to get comfortable enough on the flight home to doze long enough that we were both a bit more rested. We had four more hours until we landed, and we were really hungry for each other.

It had been chilly earlier so we were both covered by those soft bright blue blankets the airline had supplied, and we were still a bit blitzed from the drinks so frequently supplied by the accommodating flight attendants. The cabin was dark, the only illumination coming from a few reading lights. "Now that I've slept a bit," Mark whispered, "I find I'm horny as hell."

I sighed. "Me, too," I said softly. "I can't wait till we get home."

"Do we have to wait?"

"I'm not really quite up to joining the mile-high club," I said reluctantly. "Those tiny bathrooms just won't do, I'm afraid."

I felt Mark's hand slide up and down the thigh of my jeans. "I wasn't thinking of the bathroom."

"Don't be ridiculous," I said, horrified yet excited at the thought of doing it right here. And almost hungry enough to consider it. But not quite. "Not a chance, buster." His hand was probing the crotch of my jeans, rubbing and stroking through the heavy fabric. I could feel him, yet it was sort of muffled, really sexy. Playfully, I swatted his hand away. No way was I letting him paw me with a plane full of half-awake people and wandering flight attendants. "Come on, baby," I moaned. "Give a girl a break."

"You know you want it," he whispered hoarsely.

"Of course I do. But I'm not one for doing it in public, and this is about as public as it gets."

"But with this blanket over us, who'd know?"

I realized that he wasn't talking about actually fucking, just a little play. Could I?

Mark reached over and tightened my seat belt until it

was constricting my belly. He knew that things tight around my waist made me crazy. He leaned his mouth close to my ear. "What if you can't move?" he purred. "You're my prisoner, and you can't do anything about it."

God he can make me hot almost instantly. He knows me too well. I shuddered.

"Push up the armrest between us. Do it." His voice was a whisper, but the strength beneath it had me raising the armrest. "Good girl. Now put your hands on the seat beside you and don't move them."

Trembling I did as he instructed. Then I felt him unzipping my jeans and sliding his hand down my belly over my panties. "Wait," he said, pulling his hand back. "Where's your pocketbook?"

"Under the seat," I murmured, nodding to the seat in front of me.

He fumbled beneath the seat and pulled out my purse. He stared inside, then removed the small pair of scissors I always carry. "This will do nicely."

"What are you doing, you idiot?" I said.

"You'll see," he whispered, and stuffed my purse back beneath the seat. "Now put your hands back where I told you to keep them, and don't move." He reached beneath the blanket and found the opening in the front of my jeans. By feel, he placed the scissors into the leg opening of my panties and cut across the crotch. When he had completely severed the cloth, he cut up the front of the panties. He removed the scissors and dropped them in his shirt pocket. Then he pushed the crotch of the panties down between my thighs and said, "Lift up. The easier you make this, the less chance of anyone seeing."

Without thinking, I lifted my bottom off the seat, and Mark reached into the small of my back, grabbed the waistband of my panties, and pulled. With a bit of wiggling he managed to work my panties loose and pull them off completely. "That's better. I'll just hang on to these." He put the cut-up panties in his lap, beneath the blanket.

"But what will I do when it's time to get off?" I asked, half indignant and half delighted.

"Go naked underneath your jeans, I guess," Mark said, an idyllic expression on his face. "Now, where were we?" He slipped his hand into the open front of my jeans and found my pubic hair. "Ah yes." When I moved my hips, he hissed, "Don't move unless I tell you." He gazed into my eyes and knew just what buttons to push. "You're a slut and you know you like this. So sit still."

God, every time he calls me a slut, and he uses that magic word only in the heat of passion, it makes me crazy. "Yes, sir," I whispered.

A handsome male flight attendant walked down the aisle with a tray of plastic cups full of water. As he approached, Mark's finger wormed its way through my pubic hair.

"Would you like some ice water?" the flight attendant asked.

At that moment, Mark's finger found my clit. "Dear?" he said. "Water?" He rubbed, knowing I was now almost incoherent with lust.

"No, thanks," I said, choking out the words.

"And you, sir?" the attendant asked.

"Yes, please," Mark said, still rubbing. He reached out with his other hand and took a plastic cup. "Thanks."

As the flight attendant continued his rounds, Mark took a few swallows. Then he pulled his hand out of my crotch, swished his fingers in the cold water, and said, "Pull your jeans down over your hips and spread your legs as wide as you can. Do it, slut!"

His wonderful, commanding voice gave me no choice. I wiggled my jeans down, spread my legs, and closed my eyes, knowing what he was planning. Could I keep from screaming? He arranged the blanket so he had a clear path to my crotch, then took an ice cube from the water. With agonizing slowness, he moved the cube to my clit and touched me with it. Clamping my lips together so I wouldn't scream, I felt the first spasms of orgasm rock through me.

It was obvious what I was feeling so he quickly filled my pussy with his fingers, leaving the ice against my heated flesh. "Don't yell," he whispered, knowing how loud I usually am. When it appeared that I couldn't hold back, he pressed his mouth over mine, swallowing my shouts.

He kept rubbing and thrusting until I finally calmed a bit. "My turn," he whispered. Then, slightly louder, he said, "Why don't you just stretch out across the three seats and take another nap?" I raised the other armrest and lay across the three seats with my head in Mark's lap. He artfully tented the blanket so my mouth and his lap were concealed. Then he unzipped his jeans and worked his erect cock out of the fly in his shorts. "Suck it, slut," he growled softly.

Eagerly I surrounded his prick with my hot lips, bouncing my head up and down on his shaft. As I sucked, I realized he was still holding the glass of ice water. I quickly grabbed it, took a cube in my mouth, and returned to his cock. As I knew it would be, the cold of the ice against his steaming prick was just too much, and he came, filling my mouth with his come. Luckily, I was able to swallow it all or he'd have had a large wet spot on his lap.

Minutes later, we sat up and straightened our clothing. "Does that mean we're members of the mile-high club?"

"I guess we are," Mark said with a grin. "And we'll be higher still when we get home."

"I can't wait."

Atlantic City

Gamboling

ILL AND KATHY had been spending overnights in Atlantic City for many years. They found that they particularly enjoyed the poker machines and could spend hours sitting next to each other betting quarters on the outcome of each new deal. They looked over each other's shoulders as they drew to royal flushes and four or five of a kind.

Late one evening, Bill's machine dealt him the ten, jack, king, and ace of spades, and the seven of clubs. "This isn't a bad hand," he said, tapping Kathy on the shoulder.

Kathy looked at his screen and grinned. "Not at all," she said, as Bill pushed the hold button beneath the four good cards.

"It would be nice, but it's next to impossible." Although he knew it well, he looked up at the payoff list. "One thousand coins. That's two hundred and fifty dollars."

"Don't count your money yet, love."

"I'm not." His finger poised over the deal button, he said, "I know it's a long shot, but how about a bargain. If this doesn't come in, you are mine to do with what I wish for an hour before we go to bed."

"Okay, and if it does you have to buy me the best dinner in town with all your winnings."

"Done," Bill said, pressing the button. The seven of clubs became the jack of diamonds. "Ah well, at least I have a paying pair."

They played the machines for another hour, had a few good hands, and finally cashed in and headed for the elevators having lost about ten dollars between them for the evening. "Nightcap?" Bill asked.

"Nah. I had three of those delicious Bloody Marys at the machine. I'm a bit tipsy as it is."

Bill pushed the elevator button and said, "You know you owe me an hour of servitude."

"Huh?" Kathy said.

"You mean you've forgotten our bet? The royal flush earlier?"

"Oh. Right. I didn't really think you were serious."

As the elevator doors opened, Bill leered at his wife. "I most certainly was serious." He remembered a story he had read once and decided to make it come true. "I changed my mind. I don't care whether you want a nightcap or not. You're mine now for the next hour, and I get to call the shots." Bill pushed the button that would take them to the restaurant floor.

Kathy grinned and shrugged. "You masterful fool, you," she said.

They arrived at the bar and made their way to a small table in the corner. Bill ordered two Bloody Marys. As the waiter left, Bill said, "Go into the ladies room and remove your bra and panties and bring them to me."

"What?" Kathy gasped. Their sex play had frequently been delightfully creative, but this was a new twist.

"You heard me. Just do it."

"But—"

"Welshing on a bet?"

"No, but . . ." The idea was titillating but a bit scary. Because it was midsummer, Kathy was wearing a light, knit tank top and a flowing print skirt. The casino was always well air-conditioned, so she had brought along a sweater.

Bill raised an eyebrow, and Kathy stood up and walked to the ladies room. In a stall she removed her pink satin and lace bra, pulled her tank top back on over her large breasts and tightly erect nipples. She removed her light pink satin panties and put both garments into her purse. Then she walked from the stall and looked at her barely concealed body in the mirror.

Quickly she pulled on her cardigan sweater and, blushing slightly, returned to the table.

As she approached, Bill could read the arousal on her face. He looked around. There were several couples talking quietly, and a waiter and barman in conversation at the other side of the room. Before Kathy could sit down in the chair opposite him, he said, "Take off that sweater."

"Bill—"

"Do as I say," he hissed, getting a charge out of her slight embarrassment. "You're always a bit prim, except in the bedroom, of course." To Bill, Kathy really did seem to be two different people. In public she was properly dressed and made up, but in the bedroom she was an experimenter and wonderfully aggressive partner. As he thought back, Bill realized that this was the first time he'd ever "been in charge." "I won that bet fair and square. You promised."

"But there are other people here."

"We haven't been here in months and probably won't be here again for months more."

"But . . ."

To Bill's again raised eyebrow, Kathy slowly removed her sweater. Bill looked at his wife's body, his cock hardening in his pants at the sight of her large breasts revealed quite clearly through her light tank top. "When you sit down, I want you to pull up your skirt so your bare bottom is on the chair. You can do that subtly so no one else knows what you're doing."

Kathy sat down, arranging her skirt as she had been told. "That's cold," she said. She leaned over and added in a whisper, "And I'm so wet. This feels really weird."

"If you like you can put one of these napkins between you and the chair."

"No thanks."

The waiter arrived and put their drinks on the table. "Do you have anything to nibble on?" Bill asked. "You used to have those delicious bread sticks."

"We still do, sir," the waiter said. "I'll get you some."

As he left, Bill told his wife, "Give me your underwear."

Slowly, Kathy removed her bra and panties from her purse and surreptitiously handed them to Bill under the table. As she saw the waiter fill a wicker basket with bread sticks, she watched her husband spread the garments on the table. Horrified but fascinated by this new role her husband was playing, she watched the waiter walk toward the table. As the waiter held the basket out, Bill pointed to the crotch of Kathy's panties, spread on the white linen tablecloth. "Right here," he said, tapping the wisp of satin.

The waiter looked at the pink satin, then at Kathy. "Certainly, sir," he said, his expression unchanged. "Whatever you say." He put the basket on Kathy's panties.

Bill handed him a twenty-dollar bill. "We'd like two glasses of water, too."

Not knowing what else to do, Kathy sipped her drink as the waiter poured two glasses of water at the bar and returned to the table. Bill tapped his finger on her pink lacy bra and the waiter put one glass of water on each cup. "Thank you," Bill said.

"Yes, sir," the waiter said and, seeming reluctant, left. Kathy watched him quickly approach the barman and whisper to him. The two men looked in her direction and laughed.

"Now," Bill said, "skootch your chair around here next to me." There were only two chairs at the tiny table, so Kathy was easily able to move beside him, now facing the waiter and barman across the room. Bill pulled up her skirt and reached one finger into her now sopping pussy. He found her hard clit and rubbed until Kathy's hips could hardly hold still.

"Stop that," Kathy said, barely able to catch her breath. "Stop."

"What did you say?" Bill asked, rubbing more quickly. "You have nothing to say here. Sit quietly until I tell you to do something."

With shaking hands, Kathy took another sip of her drink.

While Kathy, the waiter, and the barman watched, Bill opened a package of bread sticks and withdrew a long, slender rod. "Tip your pelvis up. Do it!" As she moved, Bill broke the rod in half with obvious flourish, then reached under the table. Before Kathy could protest, he inserted the stick into her cunt. Then he resumed rubbing her clit. "You know," he said, "if you come, everyone will see. And hear, probably, since you don't climax quietly."

Kathy was almost overwhelmed by the sensations. Bill's finger rubbed her clit, and the bread stick stroked the walls of her hot passage.

"Unzip my pants," Bill hissed, "and fuck my prick with your hand."

Unable to resist, Kathy did as he instructed. She held his rigid cock, sliding her hand up and down the long, thick shaft.

"Look over there," Bill said, indicating the two employees, now watching the activities with undisguised pleasure. "They can see what we're doing. They know."

As she rubbed, Kathy watched the waiter, hidden from the view of any of the other patrons, unzip his pants and take out his cock. "Look," Bill said. "He's jacking off. I bet he's imagining it's your hand." Soon the pressure became too much, and he hissed, "I'm going to fill your hand with my come, baby." And he did.

Then, only a moment later, as she watched the waiter climax, Kathy came, biting her tongue to keep from crying out.

After a few minutes of silence, Bill rezipped his

pants and removed the bread stick from Kathy's pussy. As Kathy rearranged her clothing and put her underwear into her purse, the waiter reappeared. "Thank you, sir," he said, placing Bill's twenty-dollar bill on the table. "Thank you very much for the entertainment."

"Thank my wife," Bill said. "She's my inspiration."

The waiter looked at Kathy. "And mine." He winked, then walked back to the bar.

Bill looked at his watch. "It has been an hour, so you have paid off your wager."

"Funny," Kathy said, smiling, "I thought the bet was for two hours."

Bill grinned. "Maybe it was at that."

Music

CHOPIN FILLED her head. It flowed over her like water. No, not like water, like lava. She stood in the middle of the room full of people, but, as she looked around, they faded away. They disappeared. What was going on? For an instant she was afraid, then the lava warmth filled her and she didn't care where all the people had gone. She didn't even care what was going on.

AS MARCUS WATCHED, Diana's eyes glazed over, exactly the way he had known they would. "You see, gentlemen, now the music controls her exactly the way I explained." It had taken several months of training, using drugs and hypnosis, but now Diana's body was under his complete control. He watched her as she swayed slightly in time with the music, her deep brown eyes seeing nothing, her long, dark blond hair brushing her shoulders as she moved. Her hands were completely relaxed at her sides. As he watched, her head fell back and her eyes closed.

"Tell me how this all works," one of the men in the group asked. There were seven men, all in their late twenties or early thirties, all in full dress, standing around in the elegant living room.

"I'm afraid that's my little secret. Just let me say that Diana is at all times completely normal, charming, and intelligent, except when this music is playing. I've used the sound system here, or earphones with a Walkman clipped to her belt."

"And while she's—" the man motioned to Diana, softly swaying and seemingly in another world "—like this, she's . . . suggestible?"

"Completely. Right now she's tuned to my voice. She cannot see any of you, or hear you, unless I specifically tell her she can. I can tell her to do anything, and she'll do it. Anything. And when she awakens, that is, when the music stops, she'll remember nothing, unless I tell her to."

"Amazing."

"Remarkable."

"Is she broken in?" one man asked.

"No. Not at all. I thought whoever purchases her would like the privilege of training her."

"Hmm. Yes. That's fine. Did she agree to all of this from the beginning?"

"Yes, actually, she did. I placed an ad for a woman who wanted to be kept in luxury and wouldn't mind doing anything legal to attain that. I got hundreds of applicants, and after extensive interviews, I selected Diana and three others. Their training will be complete within a few weeks, but Diana was a perfect subject and far surpassed my expectations."

"Bring her back. I want to see how she awakens."

"Of course." Marcus walked to the CD player and changed from Chopin to Frank Sinatra.

THE CLASSICAL MUSIC was gone, and the people reappeared. Strange, Diana thought, that people should be able to appear and disappear. Oh well. She turned to the tall man who stood beside her. Hamilton. That's his name. She looked to her other side. Marcus. Yes. She had known him quite a while, but Hamilton she had met just this evening. She wondered whether this all had to do with her assignment.

Marcus had told her that she would live like a queen as long as she agreed to be her benefactor's sexual object for the occasional evening. She'd never had anything, and this was her golden opportunity. And she loved good sex. Why not get what she wanted in exchange for it.

"Mr. Hamilton," she said softly. "I'm afraid I drifted away there for a moment. What were we saying?"

"I was telling you how lovely you are."

Diana smiled ingenuously. "How could I have forgotten something so delightful? And from a man who obviously has such good taste."

Hamilton and all the other men in the room roared. "My dear," Marcus said, "you're enchanting."

Then the music played again, and she drifted away.

"MARCUS, SHE'S WONDERFUL," Hamilton said as Marcus returned from changing the CD on the stereo. "I want her."

"And so do others of us," one of the other men said. "But we'd like to see how suggestible she is."

"Of course." Marcus turned to Diana, who was obviously a million miles away, and said, "Darling. Don't you think it's warm in here?"

"I hadn't noticed it until you said it, but it is quite warm," she said, her eyes still unfocused.

"Marcus," Hamilton said, "I'd like her to be more with it. You know, I don't want a zombie."

"Diana, love, when I count to three you'll feel quite right, alive, and awake, yet you'll still hear the music and still respond to my voice and only my voice. Do you understand?"

"Yes," she said.

"One, two, three." Diana's head came up and she appeared to be completely normal. "Can you hear me?"

"Of course," Diana said.

Marcus nodded to Hamilton, who said, "And me? Can you hear me?"

Diana said nothing, nor did she indicate in any way that she heard anything. "Miraculous," Hamilton said.

"Diana, remember we were talking about how warm it is in here."

"Yes, I recall. And it's getting warmer. Maybe you should turn down the thermostat."

"Maybe you should take off the top of your dress instead."

DIANA HEARD THE MUSIC, felt the music throughout her. And she felt the lava flow through her veins, making her so warm. Small beads of perspiration formed on her upper lip and between her breasts. Take off the top of her dress. Good idea. Marcus always had such good ideas. She reached behind her, unzipped the top of her dress, and lowered it to her waist. "That's much better," she said.

THE MEN GAZED at Diana's large breasts, filling the wispy cups of her filmy lace bra. Her cleavage was deep and dark, inviting hands and mouths.

"Does that cool you off?" Marcus asked.

"Oh yes."

"Actually, it doesn't. You're still overly warm. I'll bet it's that bra. It's so hot. It's making your breasts burn and your nipples become so tightly erect." As the men watched, Diana's nipples contracted and stretched the front of the bra cups. "You need to take it off, you know."

"Of course I do," Diana said, and quickly unhooked the front clasp and removed the bra.

There was a collective sigh as the girl's magnificent breasts were revealed. Large, tipped with dark pink nipples, the breasts needed to be touched, the nipples sucked. "Who wants to play?" Marcus asked.

"I'll venture to say that we all do," Hamilton said. "She's gorgeous."

Marcus indicated Hamilton and another man, named Jacob. "Diana, your nipples are so warm, and they need something to cool them off. You can see the two men here with me, can't you?"

"Of course. They're very handsome."

The two men beamed. "They would like to help you. They have soft, wet tongues that might cool your breasts. Let them try."

Diana lifted her breasts with her hands and offered the nipples to the two men. "You have to ask them to help," Marcus said.

"Please. If you lick my nipples, I'm sure they will feel so much better."

The two men bent and licked her nipples. "That feels so good, Diana," Marcus continued. "It makes you feel so sexy. The heat you were feeling is erotic now, and it's flowing into your pussy. You can feel the heat making your pussy lips swell. Soon it's going to be hard not to invite these nice men to cool that fire also."

As all the men watched, Diana's hips started to move, and her hands fisted and unclenched. "You want to relieve that hunger, don't you? You want to touch your pussy, rub it to relieve the heat. But you can't."

"I want to," Diana said. "But I can't. What can I do?"

"Take off your dress and these two men will try to help you." Diana unzipped her dress, and it dropped at her feet. "Now your panties." Her wispy lace bikinis joined her dress on the floor at her feet. "Now sit here," Marcus said, walking over and patting the top of the bar at the side of the room.

Quickly, Diana, now dressed in only her lace-topped stockings and high-heeled shoes, lifted herself onto the bar. "It's very cool," she said.

"It's warming up very quickly from the heat of your pussy. Spread your legs so the heat can escape."

Diana spread her legs and the men all saw that her pussy was completely clean shaven. Her lips were swollen, and everyone could see how wet she was. "I have an idea," Marcus said. He moved Diana so that she was lying on the wooden surface, her spread legs toward the corners of the bar. "Now, what you want, Diana," Marcus said, "is for someone to play with your pussy. You want that very much. You also need a hard cock in your mouth, and one in each hand."

"My God, Marcus, can you have her do all that?"

"As long as the music plays, she'll do anything I want her to."

It took only a moment before Diana's body was completely occupied by the men. Hamilton was fingering her pussy. "I don't want you to put your cock into her," Marcus said. "That privilege is reserved for whoever buys her. But you can play to your heart's content."

It was only a moment before the two men whose cocks she held and the one whose erection was deeply lodged in her mouth climaxed violently. "Hamilton, would you like to come in her mouth?"

"Only when she's climaxed. Can she do that?"

"Of course. She's only waiting for my command. But maybe I should let you do that." When Hamilton smiled, Marcus said, "Diana, I want you to listen to this voice." To Hamilton, he said, "Talk to her. Tell her your name."

"My name's Hamilton, and I want you."

"His voice is as powerful as mine. You will listen to him the same way you listen to me."

As Marcus talked, Hamilton continued to play with

Diana's pussy, rubbing her clit and fucking her with his fingers. "Diana," he said, "my playing with you is getting you so excited. You need to climax, but you can't just from what I'm doing. You need my mouth to make it complete."

"Please," Diana said. "Put your mouth on me. Let me come. I need it."

Hamilton grinned. "This is amazing." He leaned over and placed his mouth against Diana's swollen, naked flesh. The men could all see his tongue lapping at her juices. "Soon, Diana," Marcus said.

"Just a few more more licks," Hamilton said. "You can come when I count to three. One . . ." He pressed the flat of his tongue against her clit and stroked. "Two . . ." He inserted the tip into her pussy and pushed it inside. "And . . ." he inserted two fingers in her hole and sucked her clit into his mouth, " . . . three."

Diana's body convulsed, great waves of pleasure crashing through her. Quickly, Hamilton moved around her body and pushed his erect cock into her mouth. Two men chuckled. "He won't even last until three. One, two . . ."

Before any of the men could get to three, Hamilton groaned as his hips convulsed.

Several minutes later, the men sat around the room alone. Diana had gone to her room to get cleaned up. "Now, how much," Hamilton said.

"Fifty thousand," Marcus said.

"And she'll want for nothing. You know that I can afford to treat her like a queen."

"Of course. I wouldn't have it any other way. She's yours," Marcus said.

"What about us?" one man said.

"I really did promise Hamilton," Marcus said. "However, I've got several more women, just as wonderful as Diana, who are finishing their training. They will be ready within the month. This evening is just a sample."

"I can't wait," several of the men said.

A Love Potion

WENDY WATCHED her husband, Matt, mix the oils. A love potion, he had told her. Was she willing to give it a try? he'd asked. Yes, she had answered. Now he was using a mortar and pestle to grind the herbs he would mix with the oils, then spread onto her body.

"God, this whole thing makes me hot," she said.

"I know," Matt said, "me, too."

"Tell me again," she said.

"Barry bought these herbs and oils in South America—some for him and his wife and some for us. He said the man told him that mixed in the proper proportions, and applied according to directions, it would make you hungrier that you have ever been. And it should work on me as well."

Wendy had heard the story several times already,

and every time she listened, it made her pussy twitch and swell, becoming wet with flowing fluids. Willing? She couldn't wait. She had never been repressed nor had Matt, but their sex life had become a bit predictable over the last few months. Something new and hot would be just the thing.

Matt reread the instructions yet again and poured some of the ground herbs into a small spoon. Then he mixed them into the oil mixture. "Are you ready?" he asked, lifting his head and nodding. "This stuff is as ready as it will ever be."

"I guess I'm ready," Wendy said.

"Okay, lie down."

Naked, Wendy stretched out on their king-size bed, her head on a pillow, her legs spread.

"I have to do this as the directions say," he said, taking a hank of soft nylon rope from a brown paper bag. With an X-Acto knife he cut it into four lengths. Slowly, he lifted his wife's right wrist and tied one end of the rope around it gently but firmly. Holding the far end, he said, "Pull. I want to make sure you can't get loose."

"Is this really necessary?" Wendy asked, making what they both knew were token protests.

"According to directions," Matt answered. "If we're going to find out whether this works, we have to follow instructions."

Wendy wiggled her rope-tied wrist. The rope wasn't tied tightly enough to cause any discomfort, but Matt's knot was secure. "Great," he said, then, as she watched, Matt tied the rope to one corner post of the headboard. He quickly did the same to her other wrist.

"Why are we doing this again?" Wendy asked, yearning to hear once more how helpless she was going to be.

"The instructions say the oil must be applied to the exact spots indicated. So just in case you wiggle and cause me to get this where it's not intended," he explained, "it suggests that you be secured to the bed."

Intent on his task, Matt tied his wife's left ankle to the leg of the bed, then rounded the footboard and grasped her other ankle. He gently widened Wendy's spread legs until they were as far apart as possible without causing her discomfort. He quickly secured her right leg to the bed frame.

Wendy lay, trying to remain calm. She wanted to rip Matt's clothes off, grab his cock, and plunge it into her, but she couldn't. She was helpless. And so hungry that she could feel her juices trickle down between her ass cheeks.

"It suggests that I make sure this isn't going to irritate, so I want to test a bit of it on your arm," Matt said. "I don't want to risk any allergic reaction or anything like that." He dipped his finger into the oil/herb mixture and rubbed a bit onto Wendy's forearm. For a full minute he stared at the slick spot in silence. "Any itching, tingling, pain? Anything unusual?"

"Nope," Wendy said, her body calming a bit as she

became accustomed to the restraints. "I don't feel a thing."

"Good. Shall we go on?"

Wendy tried not to grin too widely. "I'm as ready as I can be."

Matt again dipped his finger into the oil, gazed at his wife's mouth, then rubbed a bit on her lower lip. "That should begin to feel warm in a moment." He picked up the handwritten instructions and reread a section that Wendy thought he should have memorized by now. Spread liberally on erogenous areas, it said. Begin with the lips.

As she watched Matt she felt her lower lip get warm. To cool it, she flicked the tip of her tongue over the oil. It tasted green, like the smell of new plants in the spring. How could a taste be like a smell? Her tongue tingled. "Umm," she purred. "This feels nice. Warm and tingly."

"Really?" Matt said. "More?"

"Umm, yes."

Matt spread oil on her upper lip. Again Wendy waited a moment, then felt a warm, liquid feeling. She licked her lips and rubbed her tongue around the inside of her mouth. "Nice."

Matt grinned. Neither of them had expected this to do anything. Barry was an awful practical joker and this would be just like something he would think of. "You feel something?"

"It's hard to know whether it's the stuff or just being tied like this, but I feel very excited and very relaxed at the same time."

"Hmm," Matt said. He dipped his finger into the oil and spread a thick coating on Wendy's right nipple. Immediately she felt a tightening, and the tip became almost painfully erect. "Wow," Matt said. "Maybe this stuff works after all." He spread some on her left nipple, and Wendy watched as his eyes never left her breasts.

"Taste some," Wendy suggested.

"Good idea." He leaned over and licked the tightened nub.

Shafts of electricity speared through her. Was she really hotter than she usually was? She couldn't tell. As he licked and suckled, she wiggled against the bonds that held her immobile. She wanted, needed.

He spread more oil on her other nipple and repeated the combination of licking and sucking. It was as though there was a hot wire connecting her breasts to her clit. Her juices were flowing, and she could feel her body swell and open. "I want you so much," she moaned, struggling to get her hands free so she could grab her husband.

"Not so fast," Matt said. "We really need to test this." He covered one finger with the green goo and, with slow, deliberate motions, covered Wendy's clit with it.

"Oh God," she groaned. "That's making me crazy." It was as though all of her body had ceased to exist. The only functioning area lay between her legs. She was so hot, yet powerless to grab what she wanted.

His eyes never leaving the oily flesh between his wife's legs, Matt stood and slowly began to remove his clothes. To Wendy, it seemed to take forever as he unbuckled his belt and unzipped his pants. It took hours for him to remove his jeans and shirt, then long minutes for him to slowly pull down his shorts. "I want to know how it feels for myself," he said.

"Don't waste time," Wendy moaned. "Just fuck me."

"You're so impatient," Matt said with a grin. "I want to take my time and experience all the effects." He knelt between his wife's spread legs and rubbed the tip of his cock in the oil on her nipple. "Hmmm," he said. "You're right. It does feel warm."

Wendy thought she would come just from the stimulation of his cock on her nipple, but as she clenched her muscles and reached for orgasm, it eluded her.

"Maybe I need some of this all over my cock," Matt said. He pressed his shaft against Wendy's clit and rubbed the length of it against her.

Wendy was almost incoherent with lust. She burned for him as she never had before. "This oil is making me crazy. I need you so much."

Wendy watched Matt's face as he smiled, then nodded. "I need you, too," he said, sliding his cock into his wife's soaking cunt. He pulled back, then rammed it home again and again.

Wendy was in heaven, her cunt filled, her hips driving. When Matt pinched her left nipple she came, hard and fast, spasms rolling through her body, curling her toes and echoing through her. It seemed as if she had been climaxing for hours when she heard Matt's yell as he erupted within her. He collapsed on top of his wife and together they dozed.

ACROSS TOWN, Matt's friend Barry lay next to his wife, Jan. "I wonder whether Matt and Wendy have tried the love potion yet," she said.

"If I know Matt they have," Barry said. "That should be the end of their boring sex life."

"I didn't say that. Wendy had only complained that their sex had been getting a bit . . ."

"Boring."

"Ordinary."

Barry patted his wife's naked hip. "Well, ours is never ordinary."

Jan reached onto the bed table and wet three fingers with a green oily mixture. "Not a bit. You've got such an adventurous spirit. And this love potion is *sooo* fantastic." She spread it on Barry's swelling cock. "You know, we're running low. Do you think you'll be able to get more?" She fingered some onto her pussy lips.

It was all Barry could do not to giggle. Sure, he thought. All I have to do is get more of that heated massage oil and open a few herbal tea bags. "I should be able to," he whispered, sliding his cock into his wife's waiting pussy. The power of the mind is amazing, he thought. And with just a bit of help from his creative imagination . . . "I'm sure I can get as much as we want. And I understand there's a love-slave potion, too. Could I convince you to try it?"

Feeling Barry's cock fill her, she groaned, "Anything you like."

Coming-Out Party

*I*T HAPPENED one weekend several months ago, and I must admit that I didn't even see it coming, so to speak. Let me tell you about it.

I had been feeling particularly daring that evening and so I had worn the slip dress that I had sworn I'd never wear except with my boyfriend. Well, my boyfriend was history, and I had finally realized that I wasn't. It pains me to think of the time I wasted. For almost three months after he left, I sat in the house and mourned for what had been. Well, that night I realized that enough was enough. I was alive now. Alive and horny.

I was then, and still am, an overly sexual person who needs regular sex. I had been without it for those three months, and suddenly I decided that Marge's party was just the place to get back into the swing of things. Now

I've never been into one-night stands, but a quick, impersonal fling, I decided, would be just the thing to help me back into life. I took a long bubble bath, spent time on my makeup, and dressed in a lacy thong panty and blue stockings with lacy elastic tops. I put on the slip dress over my bare breasts and gazed at myself in my full-length mirror. I'm almost five eight, with a great figure, full breasts with prominent nipples, a slender waist, and a flat stomach. I turned and saw my tight ass beneath the medium blue, form-fitting silk. Not bad, I thought. I fluffed out my short auburn hair and slipped on my gold strappy, high-heeled sandals.

Ready or not, here I come.

The party was in full swing when I arrived, maybe three dozen people crowding Marge's large apartment. Men and women, drinks in hand, talked, laughed, flirted, and generally enjoyed themselves. I circulated, answered a few questions about my ex, and finally made my way to the bar. At my request, the bartender made me an extra-spicy Bloody Mary with two stalks of celery. As I wandered away from the bar, I caught the eye of a gorgeous guy, shaggy blond hair, horn-rimmed glasses, and a great smile. He raised his glass and saluted me with it. I smiled and raised mine and we drank together, our eyes locked across the room. He suggestively licked the rim of his glass so, the devil on my shoulder, I took a piece of celery from my drink and slowly inserted the end into my mouth, making a great show of licking the tomato juice from the tip.

His grin widened. He walked toward me, his eyes never leaving mine. "Hello," he said, his voice like warm velvet. "My name's Josh."

"Alicia," I purred.

We spent several minutes exchanging inanities, then we got fresh drinks and he took my elbow and led me toward a quieter spot in the hallway. "You're quite something," he said. "I know I should be suave and make light conversation, but I have to confess. All I can think about is how much I want you." He gazed openly at my breasts, and I knew he could see my nipples harden at the thought of his body loving mine.

I looked down at the front of his beige slacks. The fabric was stretched almost to its limits. "Yes," I purred. "I can tell."

In a flash, Josh reached behind me and opened the door to a small bathroom. Quickly we were inside and the door was shut. Josh flipped on the light and pressed the small button to lock the door. Our glasses were on the floor and his arms were around me, his mouth hot and demanding. He kept repositioning his head, deepening the kiss, devouring my mouth. His tongue plunged and backed, driving, pressing. His hands tangled in my hair, and he pulled my head back. His teeth nipped a path down my neck, and his tongue licked the hollow at the base of my throat. "God," he growled. "You're amazing."

I grabbed the back of his shirt and pulled it from his waistband. My fingers found his naked skin, and I scraped my nails down his spine. "So are you," I said, my voice hoarse, my breathing rapid. I pressed my body against his, my mouth dueling with his to further deepen the kiss. I couldn't get close enough. I dragged his jacket from his shoulders, and soon it was on the floor, along with his shirt.

He was panting as though he'd just run a marathon. His teeth found my ear, and he bit, first softly and, when I encouraged him, with a gasp, hard, causing shards of both pain and pleasure to knife through me. It was animal lust, pure and simple, and it wasn't going to be satisfied easily. But we were ready.

His hands found my tits then and his long slender fingers kneaded my hungry flesh. "Too many clothes," I growled and soon his pants and shorts joined his jacket and shirt in a heap on the white tile floor. I waited and let him grab the sides of the dress and whisk it off over my head. My panties fell on top of his clothes. "Leave the stockings and shoes. That's so sexy."

His hands were everywhere, pinching, stroking, scratching. His mouth covered my shoulders with kisses, then his lips were on my breasts, and I couldn't think, just feel. I was getting soaked, and my knees would barely hold me up as he suckled.

"Turn around, grab the edge of the sink, and hold on. Tight," he said. "We're going for a fast ride."

I needed it as quickly as he did, so I turned. My hands found the edge of the ceramic sink, and I hung on. I heard him fumble for a condom and was glad he was taking care of things. Then I felt one of his hands in the small of my back, the other in my hair. "Open your eyes and watch."

I hadn't been aware that my eyes were closed, but when I opened them I looked into the mirror over the sink. The woman who looked back at me was a tiger, hair wild, mouth open, red marks on her neck and chest. I looked up and saw that Josh was as crazed as I was. "Now see how I take you," he said.

His hands grasped my hips and his hard cock found my slippery opening. He drove into me, his balls pounding against the insides of my thighs. Reap the whirlwind, I thought, and surely a tornado was whirling through my body and my soul. His hand found my clit, and he rubbed. His teeth were on my neck, his fingers pinching my nipple.

I came. Although I tried to muffle my screams against my arm, his roar drowned out any sound I might have made.

It was several long minutes before either of us

moved. Then, in silence, both of us overwhelmed by the intensity of what had just occurred, we cleaned up and dressed.

Well, that was six months ago, and Josh and I are still together. We have a lot in common and we're never bored with each other, in or out of the bedroom. Is the sex always as cataclysmic as that first evening? Not always, but sometimes it overwhelms us both, and it's just two animals, fucking. At other times, it's long and gentle, and still others, it's playful or powerful.

I've got to go now. Josh's coming home early this afternoon, so I took the afternoon off from work. I'm wearing that same blue slip dress, and I've cleaned the bathroom. God, I love good, hot sex.

Cleopatra's Treasure

O H JOHN, it's fantastic," Lynn said, lifting the heavy necklace from its box. She held the heavy golden collar in her hand, amazed at the weight.

"It's only costume jewelry, of course," John said. "I wish it could be real."

"If it were real, it would be worth a fortune," Lynn exclaimed, "and I'd never get to wear it. Oh baby, I love it." She leaned forward and kissed her husband of fifteen years firmly on his lips. She examined the intricate bars and angles of the half necklace/half collar. "It's very Egyptian," she said, admiring the complex workmanship. Although not real gold, the piece had to have cost quite a bit.

"It's modeled after something Cleopatra suppos-edly wore," John said. "When I saw it, I naturally thought of you. I was hoping that you would dress up for me."

Lynn had a love for everything that reminded her of ancient Egypt and had quite a collection of jewelry, statuettes, and wall hangings. She also had an extensive collection of costumes. And every time she dressed up, she felt the power of the Egyptian queen course through her. She and John had some of their wildest evenings when she played queen. "Wait for me here," she said, and watched the smile spread across John's face. As she turned to go into the bedroom, she heard him get comfortable on the sofa.

In the bedroom, Lynn went to the closet and pulled out a large box. She opened the lid and withdrew a black wig, an almost-transparent dress, and a pair of two-inch platform shoes. She stripped off all her clothes, put on the wig and shoes, and took ten minutes to apply heavy makeup, with dark black outlining her eyes and lifting at the corners. Then she draped the transparent fabric around her body, fastening it with a heavy golden buckle just beneath the bosom, so it covered her yet revealed the lush outlines of her form. Then she added two gold snake cuffs to her upper arms, heavy golden earrings, and the new collar John had just bought for her.

She looked at herself in the mirror. She was strong. She was queen. She was to be obeyed.

Slowly she walked from the bedroom toward the living room, toward John.

As she entered the living room, John turned and

stared. "Oh, your highness," he whispered. "You're magnificent."

"And you are my servant," she said, her voice full and strong.

John slid from the sofa, got down on one knee, and bowed his head. "Yes, your highness."

She extended one foot. Her red-painted toes were clearly exposed between the straps of the platform shoes. "Worship me."

This was an old game for them, and she and John knew the rules well. While she watched, he put his hands behind his back and linked his fingers. He was not allowed the use of his hands, just his mouth. He knelt at her feet and kissed each toe, careful to pay no more attention to any single one than another. It was incredibly erotic to have him at her feet, but when she needed more she snapped her fingers and he stopped.

"Worship me," she said, extending her hands.

With his hands clasped behind his back, he kissed each of her fingers, then sucked each into his mouth swirling his tongue around the nail. He used his mouth as if each finger were a cock, sucking in, then drawing back. Over and over he drew the essence out of each one.

God, she was hot. It was like John's mouth was pulling the heat up from her depths and making it flow to her hot pussy. Her nipples swelled, pressing against the thin fabric of her gown. She needed his mouth, and it was hers to command. She snapped her fingers again. She watched as he sat back on his heels, gazing up at her.

She extended her arms at shoulder height and nodded. She saw John reach up with trembling fingers and unbuckle the clasp of her dress. As it opened, the slithery fabric slid from her shoulders and pooled at her feet, leaving her lush body exposed to his hot gaze. "Worship me," she said again.

In his kneeling position, John's mouth was at the height of his wife's nipples. Hands behind his back, he flicked his tongue over Lynn's erect nipples, his eyes on her body. "Let me touch you," he whispered.

"You know the rules. No slave can touch the queen." Her knees were trembling so much that she was barely able to stand, but concentrating on her balance kept the heat at bay just a bit. "Now do your duty."

With a sigh, he suckled, nursing on his wife's lush breasts. He kissed the full flesh, then nipped at the erect buds. He buried his face in the valley between them and felt her flesh press against his cheeks.

Finally Lynn knew that she had to sit down before she fell. "Enough," she said, then almost fell onto a dining room chair. She parted her thighs, exposing her throbbing pussy. She had to have his mouth. "Do it," she said.

John crawled to his wife's feet and dove quickly into

the fragrant cunt. He lapped and sucked, tasting her juices. He was so hard he wanted to loosen his pants, but he kept his hands behind his back. He licked the length of his wife's slit, then pushed the end of his tongue into her gaping hole.

Lynn slid forward until her buttocks were barely on the edge of the chair. Then she placed one foot on each side of the seat, held her knees, and spread her legs. "God, do it."

When John flicked his tongue over her clit, she trembled and felt her wetness spread to her thighs and trickle between her cheeks onto the wooden seat. He sucked the hard nub into his mouth and nibbled at the hot flesh. She shook, unable to keep her hips still. When he rubbed his chin against her inner lips while pulling on her clit gently with his teeth, she knew she was close.

He continued, knowing exactly where to suck, how to nip, when to lick. Suddenly, she couldn't hold back anymore. Pounding waves of ecstasy drummed through her body and her slave's mouth serviced her. "Don't you dare stop," she yelled, her orgasm lasting for what seemed like hours. Finally the waves slowed. Panting, she put her feet down and pushed her husband/slave away. "You were very good," she said.

"I hope so, your highness."

He had done well, her continuing tremors testimony to his talented tongue. She would allow him his pleasure. "Are you hot?" she asked.

"Oh yes, highness."

She wanted to give him something special. She thought for a moment about how best to relieve John's hunger. "Then get some oil." Yes, she thought, that will work perfectly. She had always wanted to watch him jerk off, and she suspected that he would enjoy performing for her. This was her opportunity and she knew that John wouldn't let things go further than he was comfortable with. Usually their sessions ended with his cock inside her or in her hand, but this time . . .

"Oil?"

"Get the cooking oil from the kitchen."

Quickly, John disappeared, then returned with a bottle of golden oil.

"Now strip," Lynn said, calmer.

John removed all his clothes and knelt before his queen with his erect cock bobbing, needing attention badly.

"Use the oil and show me how you play with that cock of yours. I want to watch you spurt. Kneel."

"But—"

"Are you disobeying?"

"No, but—"

She raised an eyebrow imperiously, and John uncapped the oil. He filled his palm with the slippery liquid, then placed his hand on his cock. "Oh God," he said, kneeling at Lynn's feet. "Do you really want me to do this?"

"Do you question your queen?"

John's head drooped, and his fist closed on his cock.

"Does that feel good, slave?"

"Oh yes, highness."

"Rub it. Stroke it so I can watch."

His eyes closed and his hand rubbed the length of his hard shaft.

"Faster. I want to see it come."

His hands moved faster.

"Rub your balls with the other hand."

He cupped his heavy sac with his other hand and stroked. She was getting hot again, just watching her husband pleasure himself. It was so beautiful. Although she had just had a fully satisfying orgasm, she found she was getting hungry again. She reached between her legs and touched her hardening clit. "Watch me, slave, while you do that." She gently rubbed her clit while her husband, on his knees, rubbed his erect cock and stared at her hand.

Faster and faster the two pleasured themselves until, with his head thrown back, John came, streams of thick semen arching from his cock. The sight of her husband's climax pushed Lynn over the edge, and she came for a second time.

A few minutes later, both satiated, they lay side by

side on their king-size bed. "That was so wonderful." Lynn sighed.

"God, yes," John said. "I've never done anything like that before. What gave you that delicious idea?"

"I've wanted to watch you for quite a while, but I never had the nerve to ask before."

"Ask? Cleopatra never asks. She demands. And if you have any other little ideas, your slave is only too willing to do your bidding."

"Demands . . . Hmm. I'll have to give that lots of thought."

Gift Wrap

*I*T WAS MIDEVENING, three days after Christmas, and Pam and Rick had finally gotten their lives sufficiently organized to begin the task of cleaning up the living room. Christmas paper, ribbons, tags, and boxes were strewn everywhere, but with three boys under six and endless visits to relatives and friends, this was the first chance the young couple had had to deal with the chaos.

"Lord," Pam said, opening a large black garbage bag, "this is such a mess." She grabbed a handful of red and green paper, scrunched it into a small ball, and tossed it into the bag.

"It's those kids," Rick said. "I don't know where they get their energy and how you cope with them every day. At least I go to work. It's restful there. It would be restful in a boiler factory." He took several cardboard boxes and smashed them flat, then stuffed them into the trash bag.

"It's not usually so crazy," Pam said, giggling. "The season and all the presents and food has them totally hyped."

"At least they're asleep now," Rick said, gathering more wrapping.

"Thank heavens for small favors." Pam gathered hanks of ribbon and draped them around her neck. "I can't bear to throw all this stuff away." She picked up a bow and chuckled as she stuck it to the back of her hand. "Look at me, I'm gift-wrapped."

Rick's heated glance warmed Pam's belly. "I think there's some of that great eggnog you made left over," he said. "Let's at least make this a bit more comfortable." While Pam continued to gather up trash, Rick poured two glasses of eggnog and laced each with a shot of rum.

When he returned to the living room and Pam took a taste, she said, "Are you trying to get me drunk? This is potent stuff."

"I just might be," Rick said, leering, then returning to the task of tidying up.

It took almost two hours and another glass of eggnog each for the couple to get the living room into some semblance of order. Now the gifts were neatly stacked, one pile for each member of the family, wrapping paper and boxes were ready for the trash, and Pam was festooned with ribbon.

"I'll put all this out in the morning," Rick said, tying the neck of the trash bag, "but for now I'm beat."

"Me, too," Pam said as she started to remove the yards of ribbon draped around her neck and shoulders.

"Leave that there," Rick said, "and let's go upstairs."

Enjoying the erotic glint in her husband's eye, and quite buzzed from the rum she had consumed, Pam took Rick's arm and allowed him to lead her to their bedroom. He slipped the hook on the door into the eye on the frame. "So we won't be disturbed."

"Did you have something specific in mind?" Pam asked, a look of mock innocence on her face.

"I did indeed. Now then, my Christmas present, let me unwrap you." He lifted several lengths of colorful ribbon from around her neck. Leaving a few layers of ribbon still in place, he pushed her backward onto the bed. Falling on top of his wife, Rick pressed his lips against hers softly, then, as he felt her lean into the kiss, he deepened it, probing her mouth with his tongue. "Umm," he purred. "You taste of eggnog and rum." He kissed her again.

Pam was dizzy and warm as heat slowly flowed through her body, from her lips to her breasts and her groin. As she started to wrap her arms around Rick's neck, Rick pulled back. "Actually I'd like to wrap you up a bit more tightly," he said.

That look on Rick's face usually meant that he was hatching a delightful plan. His sexual appetite was rich and varied, and his ideas always led to an evening of great lovemaking. "What are you plotting?" Pam said.

Rick took a piece of wide red ribbon and wrapped it around Pam's right wrist. Then he tied the end of the ribbon to the headboard, leaving little slack.

Pam was suddenly filled with fire. Once or twice before Rick had tied her up, and she had enjoyed it thoroughly. And each time it led to a night of erotic pleasure. But since the birth of Tony, now eleven months old, their times together had been few and far between. Praying that a little voice wouldn't interrupt them, Pam gazed into Rick's lust-glazed eyes.

Rick took a long piece of green and gold ribbon and tied Pam's left wrist to the headboard, then used silver ribbon to fasten her ankles to the legs of the bed so Pam's thighs were spread wide.

Pam wriggled and pulled, reveling in the feeling of being helpless. "This makes me so hot," she whispered.

"I know," Rick said. "It does the same to me. I love looking at you this way. Struggle some more."

Pam yanked on the ribbons until both of them were sure she couldn't free herself.

"All right," Rick said, gazing down at his now help-less wife, "I've always hated those old sweats of yours."

He disappeared into the bathroom and returned with a pair of bright silver shears. "That's why I bought you two new pairs for Christmas." He slid one side of the scissors under the elastic at one ankle and slowly cut the sweatpants up the side to the waist. Then he walked around the bed and slit the other side as well. With one pull the pants were in his hands.

"You know, I should complain," Pam said, her breathing now ragged. "Those were my favorites."

"Too late now," Rick said. He began at the waist of her sweatshirt and cut from hem to wrist on each side. Then with two more cuts up the arms, the shirt was in two pieces in his hand. As usual, Pam was braless, and her small tight breasts were crested by large fully erect nipples. Rick knelt on the side of the bed and took one tight bud between his teeth. He sucked hard, the way he knew Pam liked, then bit the pebbled tip.

"Ow," Pam said, squirming, trying to evade Rick's mouth.

"You can't get away from me," he replied, shifting his mouth to the other nipple and biting the tip.

"Shit," Pam said.

"Shh, or you'll wake the kids," Rick said. "No noise." He bit again.

Shards of fire rocketed through Pam's body each time Rick's teeth closed on her nipple. She clamped her jaws tightly to avoid shouting. Through her teeth she hissed, "You're making me crazy."

"I know," Rick said, shifting from breast to breast. "And you're helpless to stop me."

Pam was so hot she thought she would come without being touched between her legs at all, but suddenly, Rick was gone. She could hear him in the bathroom, searching through their toy box, which was hidden in the back of a high shelf in the bathroom closet. When he returned, she gasped at what she saw in his hand. The dildo was huge, one that he had bought for her a few years before as a joke.

Quickly he cut up the sides of her underpants and pulled them off. Then he wrapped a length of gold ribbon around her waist and tied it tightly. He looped another length of ribbon over the back of it and pulled the two ends down through the crack of her butt. Leaving the ends stretched out between her legs, he held the dildo where she could see it. "I'm going to fill you up," he said, "like you've never been filled."

"I don't know," Pam said, her eyes wide as she stared at the long, thick phallus.

"I do. And you can tell me to stop if you really need to." He rubbed the tip of the flesh-colored penis through her wetness, then slowly pressed it against her opening. As he pushed, he bit her nipple again. When she jumped, he pushed the dildo in a bit deeper. Over and over he bit her nipple and pushed the huge phallus more deeply into her cunt.

Pam gasped as she felt the twin sensations. The electricity of Rick's teeth and the feel of the dildo stretching her cunt were making her crazy. "Rub me," she whispered. "Make me come. Let me come. Rub me."

Rick pulled the ends of the ribbon up between her legs, imprisoning the dildo deep inside Pam's body. Then he looped the ribbon over the front of the one around her waist and tied it off, deftly keeping the phallus tightly in place.

"Mommy," a small voice called from another room. "Can I have a drink?"

"Oh shit," Pam said, sobering immediately.

Rick wiggled the dildo. "I'll get you one," he called. Then softly he added, "And you stay right here. Think about how full you are."

Rick slipped out of the room and, as Pam wiggled, moving the dildo inside of her, she dimly heard him easily caring for the boys. The ribbon was pressed against her clit, but she couldn't quite rub it the right way to let her come. And she needed to come. The hunger flooded all of her senses, heating her not quite to boiling. She pulled at her wrists, hoping she could free one hand to touch herself and relieve the pressure, but it was no use.

After almost ten minutes of torture, Rick returned. "All done," he said. "And how have you been?"

"Oh God, help me. Touch me. I'm so near, but I can't do it myself."

Rick grinned. "I know." Slowly he refastened the

door, then undressed. As he removed his shorts, Pam could see the effect that her naked body was having on her husband's cock. Hard, strong, and totally erect, it stood out from his groin. He sat beside her on the bed and held it beside her face. "This is what you want, isn't it?"

"Oh yes," Pam said. "I want you so badly."

He stroked his cock from tip to balls. "Umm," he purred. "I could come from looking at you and rubbing myself. Maybe I will."

"No," Pam hissed.

Rick went back into the bathroom and returned with a small pouch. While Pam watched, Rick reached into the fabric bag and pulled out two slender chains with clips attached. "Remember these? Remember how crazy they used to make you?"

Nipple clamps. They hadn't played with those in years. Early in their marriage, Rick had discovered how sensitive his wife's nipples were and how they seemed to control her entire sexual reaction. Pam remembered that on several occasions Rick had clipped the clothespin-like objects to her nipples, then put an oversize shirt on her and made her walk around the house. The brushing of the cloth across the clips moved then just enough to keep her bathed in lust. She had all but attacked him. Now, as hot as she already was, she could do nothing to make herself come and nothing to stop him from stoking the fire with those clamps.

Several times he snapped the clips, then slowly he attached one to her right nipple. The effect was electric. Pam could feel the flood of her juices around the dildo, still buried in her pussy. She bucked her hips trying to use the ribbon against her clit to make herself come. When Rick attached a clamp to her left nipple the effect was doubled. Tripled. Multiplied by a hundred. She couldn't hold still. She alternately arched her back and raised her hips, reaching for something she couldn't get.

"Open," Rick said, tapping her mouth with his cock. "Do it."

She gladly opened her mouth and took all of his hard cock inside. She flicked her tongue over the tip, then licked the length of his shaft. She sucked it in slowly, then pulled her head back, creating the suction she knew he liked. Faster and faster she worked on his shaft until she could feel his orgasm build. "I can't touch your balls," she said, "so you do it. I want your hands to help me make you come."

Rick slid one hand around the base of his cock and stroked his balls. It took only a moment until Pam felt spurts of hot come fill her mouth. Unable to swallow it all, she felt some of the thick fluid dribble from the corner of her mouth.

"Oh baby," Rick whispered. "That's so good."

Moments later, Rick was between Pam's legs, twisting the dildo, then moving the ribbon so he could take her throbbing clit into his mouth. He sucked and nibbled until, in only seconds, Pam came, waves of orgasm overwhelming her, taking her breath.

It took several minutes before either of them could speak. Panting, Pam finally said, "That was the best Christmas present I've gotten in years."

Rick used the scissors to cut the lengths of ribbon from Pam's body. "Well, I certainly enjoyed wrapping it."

Just a Guy and a Girl

YOU'LL NEVER FIT the car into that space," Jena said to her husband.

"Come on, there's lots of room. I could get two cars into that." Walt pulled their Ford up next to the Toyota in front of the tiny empty space at the curb.

"Never."

"Put your money where your mouth is," Walt said.

"Okay," Jena said, a gleam in her eye. "But no money. You've got three passes to get the car into the space. If you can do it, and I'm sure you can't, you get me for an hour of servitude. And if you don't park it properly, within a foot of the curb, I get you. For an hour. Whatever I want to do. Bet?"

"Bet." Walt shifted the car into reverse, backed up and cut the wheel. After three passes, he shifted into park and said, "Okay. Done."

Jena opened her door and looked at the curb. "It's not parked, it's abandoned. It's at least a mile from the curb."

Walt got out and, much to his dismay, even he had to admit it was at least two feet away. "Hm. How about one of Shaq's feet?"

"Not a chance. So now you're mine. Tonight. For one hour." Jena grinned, then got out of the car, and Walt watched his wife disappear into the crowd.

That evening, they put the children to bed, went into the bedroom, and Jena locked the door. "Okay, baby, now you belong to me for one entire hour." She placed the oven timer she had brought with her on the dresser and set it for the required time. "Now," she snapped, "strip. We're going to play a game."

Jena had given the evening a lot of thought. She had a good idea of her husband's deepest fantasy, and tonight she was going to make it come true. She also knew that he would stop her if she went too far. They trusted each other completely.

Walt looked at his wife and grinned. Their sex life had always been adventurous and creative. As he pulled his T-shirt off over his head, he wondered exactly what she had in mind. Never mind, he told himself. It would undoubtedly be fantastic. He slipped off his shoes and removed his socks. Then he opened his jeans and pulled them and his shorts off. Naked, his erection hard and sticking straight out from his groin, he stood, watching his wife's eyes roam over his body.

"Tonight, we are going to change roles. You're going to become a girl, and I'll be the guy. You get to go first. I'm going to change you into a beautiful woman."

"Hey now, wait a minute," Walt said.

To Jena's ear, his protests were not quite convincing. Over the years of their marriage, Jena had watched her husband go from mildly curious to wildly fascinated with women's apparel and makeup. He loved to watch her put on her eyeliner, foundation, blush, and lipstick. Often he would sit on the bed as they prepared to go out, his eyes never leaving her legs as she put on her stockings. So now, she was going to give him the full treatment. "No, you wait a minute. Are you welching? We had a bet, you remember." She looked at his cock, sticking straight out from his groin. "You can't lie to me. You're excited, and you're going to be more so as I create the new you."

"Yeah, but—"

Jena stared at her husband and raised a questioning eyebrow. His mouth closed, and he rested his hands in his lap. Jena rummaged in her bureau drawer and found an old, stretched-out pair of panty hose. She took a pair of scissors and cut a hole in the front. "Now put these on."

Walt was slight, of slender build, so Jena knew the hose would go on with only a bit of difficulty. She watched as Walt held the stocking in his hand, staring at the flesh-colored nylon. She watched the indecision wash over his face, then she saw him make up his mind. He sat down on the bed and stuck his toe into the right stocking leg.

"Not that way," Jena said. "You've seen me do that lots of times. Like this." She knelt at his feet and scrunched the right panty hose leg onto her thumbs. Then she nodded and Walt stuck his toe into the opening. Slowly Jena drew the tight nylon up his leg, to just above the knee. Then she repeated the process with his other leg. "Stand up." As she pulled the hose up the rest of the way she watched as his cock twitched and pre-come leaked from the tip. She had been right. This was driving him crazy.

"You know," she said as she stepped back to look at her handiwork, "for next time, I'll have to get some other things for you to wear. Maybe a large bra. You'd look so wonderful." Her mind racing, she finally thought of a pair of baby-doll pajamas that she hadn't worn in several years. While Walt watched her every move, she found them in her closet and held the top out for him to see. "For tonight, we can put this on you."

Walt was silent and immobile, obviously unable to control his body. "Arms up," Jena said and slowly Walt's arms lifted. She slipped the white nylon pajama top over his hands, down his arms, and over his head until the straps were on his shoulders and the floaty fabric covered his chest. Jean stroked her husband's belly, shoulders, and back through the smooth material, noting his breathing quicken, his hands tremble. "Mmm," she crooned, "so smooth. So soft."

"Oh Lord," Walt groaned. "Oh Lord."

Jena glanced at the timer. She still had about half an hour. They spent the next fifteen minutes in the master bathroom as Jena used all her makeup to create a woman's face on her husband's body. "Beautiful," she said finally.

"Oh baby."

"Now we need to complete this sexual swap. Go inside and wait for me." She closed the bathroom door and sighed. About two months earlier she had ordered several sex toys from a catalog and, for some reason, she had ordered a harness and a selection of dildos. She had put them into her toy bag in the bathroom closet and left them there. Had she known this evening was coming?

Now she quickly stripped. Her nipples were hard, her pussy soaked. This entire situation was making her incredibly hot. She fit a slender dildo into the harness's opening and slid a second, heavier dildo into her sopping pussy. "Very clever," she muttered as she fit the rest of the harness on, fastening heavy leather straps around her hips and pressing the base of the artificial penis against her clit. She could feel the throb of her excitement as her clit was stimulated and the thicker dildo filled her cunt, held in place by the harness straps. A slender rod now stuck out from her groin. She took a deep breath, opened the bathroom door, and stepped out.

Walt had been staring at the door and now just sat, unmoving, his eyes wide, his breathing so loud she could hear it across the room.

"My lovely girl needs a good fucking," Jena said.

Slowly and silently, Walt rose to his feet.

"Bend over," Jena said, walking up to him. She turned him around and pushed him so he was bent over the bed, his ass in the air. She took the scissors and snipped a hole in the rear of the panty hose. "Now, my sweet girlie, you will get a good fucking." She grabbed a tube of lubricant from her bedside table and applied a large dollop to the dildo. "But I must be sure my girlie is ready." She put another big dollop on her hands and rubbed it around his asshole, penetrating only a half inch. Her penis would do the rest of the job quite well. The dildo in her pussy made her knees shake, and she knew that with just a few thrusts the clit stimulator would make her come.

Slowly, Jena pressed the tip of the slender dildo against Walt's opening and pushed.

"Oh no," Walt said as the rod penetrated his virgin rear. "Oh no." But to Jena's ears, the sound was not a negation, but an affirmation. And she knew that he would use their safe word if he really wanted her to stop.

"Oh yes, girlie," Jena said. "Oh yes. You need a good fucking." She pushed gently but steadily, and inexorably the dildo penetrated Walt's rear. As she pushed, her clit rubbed against the plastic clit tickler, and the dildo moved inside her cunt. She pulled back, then pushed, simulating fucking. In and out as the sensations in her pussy drove her higher.

Her hand still slippery from the lubricant, Jena reached around and grabbed Walt's cock. Shaking with impending orgasm, she rubbed. "Baby," Walt yelled as his cock erupted, spilling gobs of hot semen on the bed. Jena kept thrusting as the clit stimulator rubbed and she felt the orgasm explode in her belly. "Yesss," she hissed. "Yesssss." The orgasm went on and on, then finally calmed.

She pulled out, and the two lovers collapsed onto the bed, panting.

Later, they showered together and climbed between cool sheets. "I'm not gay," Walt said.

"Of course you aren't," Jean said. "That was just fun to play with, just you and me."

"Just you and me?" Walt said.

"Right. Just a guy and a girl indulging in good sex together."

"Yeah," Walt said, grinning. "Just a guy and a girl." They cuddled together and fell asleep.

Tennis

I THINK it was her legs that got me. I love strong, well-developed legs, and as I watched her about to serve at forty-fifteen, I knew I was in love. No, actually I was in lust. I sat down at a small table beside the court and put my gin and tonic on the table in front of me.

As I knew she would, she tossed the ball, then raised her racket over her head, prepared to swing. Her breasts pressed against the stretchy fabric of her shirt, and I was sure I could see the large nipples outlined against the material. She swung and I was in heaven. So I sat, waiting for my friend Jack to join me for singles, and just stared. I propped my chin on my hand and closed my eyes, imagining she was mine.

. . .

SUDDENLY, we were alone on the court and it was twilight. "What's your pleasure?" she asked, her voice husky and deep. She was still wearing the white knit shirt and short tennis skirt.

"You are," I said. "Come here." She did, and I pressed her against my now hard cock. God, I wanted her so badly. I looked at her mouth, soft, warm, slightly open, then pressed my lips against it, teasing, tasting. I licked her lips and watched her head fall back. I ran my tongue over the pulse in her throat, then blew on the wet trail, enjoying her body's obvious reaction.

"You're mine tonight," I said.

"I know," she whispered.

There was a chain-link fence surrounding the court, and I slowly walked her backward until her spine pressed against the cold steel. "Feel good?"

"Oh yes," she purred.

I grabbed her wrists and stretched her arms over her head against the fence, pressing and holding her against the cold steel. I felt her hips buck and I saw her lips reach for mine. "That excites you, doesn't it?"

"Yes," she hissed, her breath whooshing out between her teeth.

There were silk scarves in my hands, and I quickly tied her wrists to the links, just tightly enough that she couldn't get away. Her eyes were hot, her mouth open. "Spread your legs," I ordered, and she stepped out as wide as she could. More scarves tied her ankles. Now she was truly mine, comfortable yet unable to move more than an inch in any direction. My cock ached to be inside of her, but I had a lot to do first.

"You're a problem, my love," I said. "You make me too hard to wait. But I have a cure for that." I unzipped my shorts and pulled out my hard-on. I wrapped my hand around it and slowly began to stroke along its length.

"No, don't do that," she moaned. "It's mine. It should be inside my pussy."

"Later," I said. "He will be deep between those gorgeous legs soon enough, but he has to have something now." I rubbed and, in only a moment, semen boiled inside of me and erupted onto the asphalt at her feet. God, it was good, and the sight of her eyes, staring at my cock, made it so much better. I wanted to sit and just enjoy the afterglow but there was going to be so much more. "Now we have some time."

A bag awaited me on the ground a few feet away, and inside I found a pair of scissors. "First," I said, "you're wearing many too many clothes." With slow precision I cut up the front of her shirt, then out through both sleeves until I could pull the shirt off. Now her almost naked back was pressed against the cold links of the fence. "How does that feel?"

"Cold." She trembled, from a combination of the cool air on her skin and her lust for me. It was as though I could read her thoughts as she looked at me with hot eyes. She wanted me. But not yet. We had a long way to go.

With one snip her sports bra parted. Two more snips, and the straps were severed and it was in my hand. I stared at her nipples, so large and fully erect, her breasts lifted as her arms remained immobile above her head. I leaned over and flicked my tongue over the deep brown tips, watching them almost reach for my mouth. "I know what you like, you know," I said. I took a pair of suckers from the bag at my feet and quickly attached them to her wet nipples. I watched her writhe and squirm with pleasure as the suction devices tugged at her overheated flesh. "Tell me."

"Hot, so hot. They feel like your mouth sucking on my tits, both at the same time. It's almost too much."

I smiled. "Almost."

She looked at me, then closed her eyes.

Next, I cut off her skirt and the attached stretchy panties until she stood revealed to me. I placed my palm against her belly and pushed, forcing her buttocks against the cold fence. She jerked and moaned, tossing her shoulder-length hair from side to side as she almost writhed with the pleasure of it.

Again I reached into the bag, and this time I withdrew a length of slender chain. I wrapped it around her waist, fastened it with a small padlock, and moved it around until the lock was in the small of her back, the remaining length of chain hanging almost to the ground, cold between her butt cheeks.

She was almost incoherent with lust, but thanks to my earlier masturbation, I could wait . . . and watch. I pulled a large dildo from the bag. "Open your eyes," I said.

Slowly her lids rose, and I held the oversize artificial penis in front of her face. "You know where this is going, don't you?"

"Oh no. That won't fit." It was bright red, probably nine inches long and more than two inches in diameter, with a ring at the blunt end.

"Yes, it will. I know how hot you are, and I know you can take it all." I bent over and rubbed the tip of the cock against her soaked pussy. As I had known it would, it slipped inside her easily, yet I knew it stretched her in the most delightful way. When it was lodged deeply within her, I pulled the hanging length of chain between her legs, threaded it through the ring, and fastened it to the chain at her navel with another small padlock. She moaned and bucked her hips, trying in vain to hump the dildo, trying to make it fuck her the way she wanted, needed.

"Now the fun begins. You know I love to tease you, baby," I said. "I love it when you're so close to coming that you beg, but you know I won't let you." I pulled a small box from the bag. "Well, I will let you, eventually."

I knew every detail of how the device worked. There was a nob that protruded from the side of the blunt end of the dildo and slowly revolved around the thick rod, rubbing against the sensitive areas just inside a woman's passage. I turned a small dial on the box. She went wild, rotating her hips, trying to get more of the dildo to move, to satisfy her lust. I listened as her body's movements made the fence clang and rattle. She was beyond caring about the noise. "Please," she moaned. "You're driving me crazy."

I smiled. There was still one more goodie, a tickler, a hidden rod that could slide from the blunt end and slowly massage a woman's clit. I pressed the lever now to activate it.

I knew she was close, but each time she was ready to drive herself over the edge, I slowed or stopped the motion of the delightful device lodged deep in her cunt. Over and over I pushed her to the brink, and each time I backed her off, until sweat was running down her body and my cock was hard again. With a tiny key I removed the lock at her navel and released the chain. I cut the scarves that held her ankles, leaving her arms pressed against the fence.

I quickly stripped and put on a condom. I wanted the freedom to do as I pleased. And I knew what I pleased. I grabbed her ankles and draped her knees over my arms so her ass hung free against the fence.

She loved to be ass fucked, and I was going to finish this in my favorite way. I rubbed my covered cock in the juices that ran freely down the insides of her thighs. Then I rubbed my hard dick around the rim of her hole, and slowly pressed it into her. Ever so gradually my cock entered her rear passage, made tighter by the huge dildo still lodged inside of her. "Oh yes, baby," she cried. "Fill me up. Please, do me hard."

Hard it was. I rammed my cock up as far as it would go, then turned the two parts of the device up full. I could feel the nob as it rubbed against her passage and thus against my cock. I wanted to wait, but it was no use. With a bellow, I came again, my cock pounding into her. I reached between us, wiggled the dildo and rubbed her clit. She screamed, a long, loud noise that would have awakened the dead. "Yes, yes, yes," she cried. "Yessssssss."

"HEY BUDDY," a voice said. "Are you asleep?"

I jerked upright, my wrist sore from supporting my head. "Oh shit," I said, swiveling my head to see Jack standing above me.

"Long day?" he asked.

"I guess." Still scrambled, I tried to hold on to the vision of the woman as she came, but as with most dreams, it was already fading.

"That's game, set, and match," a voice yelled from

the court. "Nice game, Terry, but not good enough
yet."

"Hey, ladies," Jack yelled. "If you're not too tired,
how about a set of doubles?"

"Sure," one said. The one with the breasts and the
incredible legs. "My name's Terry and that's Paula.
Which one of you is the better player?"

"Actually I am," Jack said, "so since you're the win-
ner, you take Jake, and I'll play with Paula. We'll show
you two how tennis is really played."

I watched all of this, the fog rapidly lifting. I
grabbed my racket from the bag at my feet. Looking at
the bag brought back shards of my foggy dream.
Dream? Maybe. But could it happen? I ran out onto the
court. "Hi. I'm Jake."

She reached out her hand. "Hi." We shook. "We can
volley for serve." She winked at me. "And loser buys
drinks afterward."

The Power of Love

ROB AND CASSIE had been married for seven years. Although they were planning on having a family eventually, they both worked and were willing to wait.

One Saturday evening they were sitting in their living room, amazed that they had no social plans. "What would you like to do this evening?" Cassie asked. "We could see what's at the movies."

"I'd prefer to stay home and fool around all evening," Rob said, leering at his wife and twirling an imaginary mustache.

"Mmm," Cassie said, snuggling close. "Sounds good to me. How about a bubble bath?"

Rob took a deep breath and mentally crossed his fingers. "I had something different in mind."

"Oh?" Cassie looked at her husband. "You look serious. What's up?"

Again Rob filled his lungs with air and let his breath out slowly.

"Come on, babe," Cassie said. "Tell me. Is something bothering you?"

"Things have been real good in the bedroom department recently and, well . . ."

Cassie sat silently, waiting for Rob to tell her what was going on.

Finally he said, "I've had a fantasy for, well almost forever, and I'd like to play. But I don't know how to discuss it or whether you'd be interested."

"Go on," she said softly.

Rob turned so he couldn't see Cassie's face as he revealed his deepest desire. He trusted her to be honest with him, yet not hurt him as he took a risk, telling her something so difficult. "I don't think I ever told you that I got into hypnosis in high school. I got pretty good, actually."

"No, you never told me. Did you do the cluck-like-a-chicken stuff? I've always thought that was a bit much."

"No, I never embarrassed anyone like that. But I did have fun at parties with people who were willing to play." He swallowed hard and again mentally crossed his fingers. "Would you be willing to play?"

"You mean let you hypnotize me? I guess. Do you think you remember how?"

For weeks, Rob had been contemplating approach-

160 *Joan Elizabeth Lloyd*

ing Cassie with this idea, so he had been poring over his old books on the subject. He had even gone to a bookstore on his lunch hour to get a few new ones. He remembered everything. "Yes, I still know how, but your 'I guess' isn't good enough. I'd be interested only if you were one hundred percent willing. I'd want your complete cooperation."

Rob still faced away from his wife, but from her long silence, he could imagine Cassie thinking about what he had proposed. He had wanted to play for as long as he had had sexual fantasies. Hypnotize a woman and have her under his control. He got hard just thinking about it now. But it had to be a cooperative thing.

"It sounds exciting," Cassie said finally. "Is it true that you can't make someone do something they don't really want to do?"

Rob turned toward his wife and looked deeply into Cassie's eyes. "Whether I can or can't, you'd have to trust me completely not to do anything you didn't want. I know you well, in and out of bed, and I just want to have some fun. I'd never do anything that you wouldn't enjoy."

Cassie smiled. "I do trust you, babe. Let's try it. What do I have to do?"

Rob sighed and grinned. "Really?" Was it really going to be this easy? Why hadn't he suggested it years ago? he wondered.

Cassie giggled. "Yes, really. This is something you

really want, and the idea turns me on, actually. I would be kind of a sex slave. Kinky. Can I make one request? I've seen this stuff on TV and they sometimes make the person in the trance forget what went on. Don't make me forget what we do. Okay?"

Rob's grin widened. "Not a chance. You will remember everything and so will I." He got up and disappeared into the bedroom, then returned with a candle. He lit it, set it down on the coffee table, then turned out all the lights. "Sit comfortably and put your hands on your thighs. Just look at the candle and relax. Take a deep breath and relax."

Rob watched his wife put her hands on her legs and visibly relax. "I want you to feel the heat of the candle in your fingers," he said, his voice low and soothing. "They will feel it first, since they are close to the candle. Do you feel the heat?"

"Yes."

"Good. The heat is very relaxing. It travels up your arms and now you can also feel it in your knees and thighs. Does it feel good?"

"Yes."

"Warm and soft and comfortable."

"Yes," Cassie said, her breathing deepening.

The litany returned to him like riding a bicycle. He had done this often in high school, and now all the moves and words rushed back into his head. But this time it was also different. This time it was his wife, and he was going to do things with her that he hadn't had the nerve to do before. "That's fine. As that heat flows through your legs and arms, they get so relaxed. The heat is so relaxing. Feel it flow through your arms and legs, and now into your belly and chest. You feel almost heavy, yet totally relaxed. It's warm and comfortable, washing over you. Tell me how you feel."

"I feel good," Cassie answered, her voice thick, her breathing deep. "Relaxed and good. Warm."

"Wonderful. That's just right. Now the heat flows into your neck and face. As it flows to your eyes, they want to close because you're so relaxed. It's all right if they close. That just makes you feel more relaxed." He watched his wife's eyes slowly close. "Good. Very good. Are you feeling very relaxed?"

"Yes."

"Good. And every time you say the word *yes*, you get even more relaxed. You know you're being hypnotized, don't you?"

"Yes."

"And you are enjoying it?"

"Yes."

"Good. You feel all warm inside, and that warmth is relaxation. Now, are you willing to play with me?"

"Yes," Cassie said softly. "I want to play with you."

"Okay. You can open your eyes. And with your eyes open, you'll be even more relaxed." He watched

Cassie's eyes slowly open. "I want you to be my sex kitten. Can you do that?"

"I don't know how," she said slowly.

"I will teach you. But being my sex kitten is the most wonderful thing you can think of being. Is that right?"

Cassie smiled. "Oh yes. That would be wonderful."

He had fantasized about this so often that he knew exactly what he wanted. First he had to make her feel sexy and hot. "How would a sex kitten look, do you think?"

"She'd have big tits and a tiny waist. She'd have long hair all the way down her back."

"If that's how you think you should look, we will make that happen."

"We will?"

"Yes. Stand up and undress. It's comfortable for you to do that. And as you shed your clothing, you'll also shed any shyness you have. You are a sex kitten, and sex kittens aren't shy about anything."

Cassie stood up and, as Rob watched, slowly removed her shirt, jeans, shoes, and socks, then her bra and panties. She stood, gloriously naked, her shoulders back, her breasts thrust forward. She looked anything but shy. "You don't think you look like a sex kitten?"

Cassie looked down. Rob had always loved his wife's body, but he knew that she wanted her breasts to be bigger. "No."

"Come into the bedroom," he said, and she dutifully followed him. "Now look at yourself in the mirror. You are a sex kitten, but you need some special clothing." He and Cassie had bought some sexy lingerie from a catalog a while back and had had an evening of hot sex when she first wore bits of the outfit. But now it had lain in the drawer for months. He found a black waist cincher with no bra cups and a pink ribbon up the front. He wrapped it around her waist and fastened the dozen hooks up the back. "Now look at yourself," Rob said. "Amazing things will happen as I pull the ribbon tighter." He grasped the ends of the pink satin. "As I pull, your waist will get smaller and your breasts will grow. I'm going to pull just a bit now. Tell me what you see."

"Oh," Cassie gasped. "That's wonderful. My tits are so big now. And my waist is much smaller."

"I'll pull again and it will happen still more." He pulled.

"Oh." Cassie cupped her breasts and held them in her hands. "Oh."

"Now one last pull. With that one, your hair will get longer and turn deep black, too." He pulled one last time. "Then you will look just like a sex kitten."

"Oh it's so wonderful."

"Now that you're a sex kitten, I want you to kneel before me. And as your knees touch the carpet you will be even more relaxed. You will see only me, and you will believe me to be the sexiest man you've ever seen."

He watched as his wife knelt at his feet. This was his fantasy come true, and with his own wife. "Now I'm wearing some very sexy clothes, but you must remove them. They are getting in the way of your seeing me. Now take them off."

Cassie reached out and unzipped Rob's jeans. "So beautiful," she said as Rob's hard cock sprung free. Her breathing quickened as she gently touched his cock with the tip of her index finger.

"But the rest of my body is sexy, too. And as you remove each piece of my clothing, you will get more relaxed, but hotter, hungrier. First my shirt." He gradually instructed her to remove all his clothing until he was naked.

"Now kneel again, and remember that each time you kneel down you get more deeply into that wonderful relaxed place." She did. "Now you want nothing more than to touch my cock. Take it in your hand and stroke it." Until then he had been able to hold his excitement in check, but with his wife's hands fondling his cock and balls, he suddenly realized that he was rapidly losing control. "Okay, stop now." He could wait.

Cassie settled back on her haunches, her hands resting on her thighs. "Now you are so hungry for me it's hard to wait. Are you wet?"

"Oh yes."

"Touch it." Cassie reached between her thighs and wiggled her finger into her crotch. "Show me."

Cassie wet her finger and extended it so her husband could see. He licked the moisture from the tip. "Good. But we need to make it easier. You'll be much more comfortable on the bed." It took only a moment until Cassie was lying, spread-eagled. "Now touch it where it's hot." He loved to watch as Cassie occasionally masturbated while they made love, but she was usually in a hurry to feel his cock inside. In his fantasy he could watch her as long as he wanted. And this was his fantasy. "Touch it." Cassie's hand worked between her legs, rubbing, making circles over her clit. "Can you come that way?"

"Yes."

"Good, do that. I want to watch you come." As he watched, Cassie's eyes closed and her fingers flew. Suddenly Rob watched her back arch and her breathing almost stop. "If you want to scream, it's all right. It will feel natural." She was always silent when she came but now, he knew, she needed the outlet.

Cassie yelled as her hands worked and her body spasmed. Rob loved it. She was so beautiful when she came. So beautiful. And he was so hot and his cock so hard that it almost hurt. Now he wanted to watch his wife's beautiful hands on him. He waited until her breathing slowed. "Are you calm now?" he asked.

"Yes," she said, softly.

"Well, you need to touch me now. My cock needs your hands." He knelt on the bed so she could reach him without moving. He watched her reach out ever so slowly until he felt her hands caressing his hard, erect penis. And he wanted to come. "Faster," he said, and with his encouragement she found his rhythm. He had seen come shots in XXX-rated films, and he had wanted to come on his wife's face for a long time. Now he would do it. "Yes," he whispered. "Yes." Come boiled from his balls and erupted from his cock, spurting onto his wife's beautiful cheeks. "Open your mouth," he said, and the second spray found her spread lips. "Lick it." She did, her soft pink tongue snaking out and finding the gobs of thick, white fluid. God, Rob thought, it's another of my fantasies. So good.

It was long minutes before he finally calmed. Then he wet a small towel in the bathroom and slowly washed Cassie's face. Finally he said, "Now I will tell you a word that will put you back into this trance whenever we want. Marshmallow. When I say 'marshmallow' your eyes will close and you will be back in this wonderful place where you are now. Do you understand?"

"Yes," she said, still lying on the bed.

"And when I clap my hands, you will be awake. And you will remember everything that happened." He clapped and watched the subtle changes in Cassie's body that signaled to him that she was no longer hypnotized.

"Phew," she said. "That was amazing."

"Do you remember everything?"

"I think so. I came so hard that I'm exhausted. So good. I watched you come. That was great."

"I gave you a word that will put you back there. If you want, I will remove that part, and I won't ever do this again." Rob was amazed at how disappointed he would be, but this had to be her decision.

"I loved it. It felt good. But it's our secret. No one else is ever to know."

"Absolutely."

"And if I decide I don't want to do this again, we won't. Right?"

"Right. I love you and would never do anything you didn't want."

"Good. And what was that word again?"

"Marshmallow."

Cassie smiled and sighed and closed her eyes.

A Shower Massager

PHIL ARRIVED at his motel late in the evening. He was beat. Seven hours of driving and then, when he'd gotten off the interstate, he'd gotten thoroughly lost. Now it was almost nine and he was hungry, tired, and very cranky.

He'd left later than he'd planned that morning. Carol had been so gorgeous, lying in bed wearing a nightgown that just drove him crazy. He'd showered and dressed, vowing this time to get an early start. But when he bent over to kiss her good-bye, she'd put his hand on her breast. Soft and firm, covered with that satiny fabric that slithered and slipped and almost flowed beneath his hand. He had felt her nipple harden, and he'd been a goner. It had taken almost two hours before both of them were satisfied.

Then another shower, breakfast, hours of driving with

a drive-through burger for lunch. What a way to spend a Sunday. But he was here now, and ready for his eight o'clock meeting the following morning. Bright eyed and bushy tailed. That's what he'd be in the morning. Just a few minutes to hang up his clothes so they wouldn't look like he had slept in them, and a quick bite at the diner next door. Then a good night's sleep and he'd be ready.

He opened his suitcase and there, on top, was a small, gift-wrapped package. Inside the silver paper he found a small tape player, with a tape already inside. He pushed play and heard his wife's familiar voice.

"Hello, darling.

"I miss you so much already, and I wish you didn't have to be away from me so much of the time. This traveling you do is so hard on both of us. And what's a poor horny woman to do? You know I won't ever cheat on you, but I'm hungry. All the time. So I've learned how to handle it myself. Get it? Handle? I thought you'd enjoy my little play on words.

"With you away so much of the time, I'm developing new ways to please myself, and I thought you might want to hear about one I think will be *sooooo* good."

Phil set the player on the table beside his bed. He stretched out on the spread and crossed his ankles. Dinner could wait. After all, the diner was open twenty-four hours, and listening to his wife's sexy voice was causing him to develop a different kind of hunger.

"I'm recording this on the Wednesday of last week

when you were away. Remember how we talked on the phone and almost made love through the wires that night? I came, rubbing my pussy while you stroked your cock, so far away."

Phil smiled. He remembered that evening well. They'd stayed on the phone for almost two hours and he'd gotten almost no sleep. Fortunately that meeting had gone well in spite of him.

"I know that the phone bill for that evening was so enormous that we've vowed to talk only once for each trip, and then for only a few minutes. But what good is that? How can a girl get off that way? Well, I've found other ways, and I thought you should know about a few of them.

"You know what I like best? Well, I'm going to run a big tub full of hot water and I'll be back."

Phil heard a few moments of silence, then a snap on the recorder. Then his wife's voice began again.

Did you miss me? I filled our big bathtub with hot water, and now the recorder is siting on the sink beside the tub. I'm in the water, all naked. I've got the soap in my hands, and I'm rubbing up a good lather. The soap is so slippery as I rub my hands over it. So slippery."

Phil could hear the sound of water sloshing. He could picture his wife's body, lush and full. No skinny women for him. Soft, curvy, with lots of flesh he could knead and stroke. He moaned low. Thinking about his wife's body was making him hard.

"I'm rubbing the lather over my breasts now," her voice continued. "All over, but I'm not touching my nipples. They are all pointed and tight because they are wet from the bathwater and cold from the chill air. But I've got the space heater blasting for what I want to do later so I'll be warm soon.

"I'm looking at my tits as I rub soap on my ribs. You love my breasts, don't you? They are very white with tan lines where my bikini ends. Dark tan, white skin and dark, hard nipples.

"I think they need my fingers now, so I'll lather my hands again. Hard, slippery soap. Remember when we made love in the tub a few weeks ago? I lathered your cock then with my soapy hands."

Phil remembered. He unzipped his jeans and rearranged his shorts so his hard cock could get some room. He remembered.

"I'm rubbing my tits now, but I wish these were your hands. Pinching my tight little buds. Swirling around my white skin. Cupping my big globes. I'm stroking my ribs and belly now with one hand, while the other is busy with my tit. God, this feels good."

Phil's breathing quickened as he listened to his wife's voice. He heard the tape being shut off, then starting again.

"Did you wonder where I went? Well, I've let most of the water out of the tub. The heater has really helped, so the room is steamy-hot. I've taken the shower massager from down from the pole and I have it in my hand. I'm turning on the water. Shit," she hissed, "that's cold." There was a pause. "That's better," Carol said.

Phil grinned and opened the fly of his shorts to allow his erection to spring free.

"I'm turning the nozzle to pulse and spraying the water on my tits."

Phil could hear the water as he pictured his wife lying naked in the tub.

"God that feels so good. It's like dozens of tiny fingers playing with my nipple. I'm adjusting the spray so it's needle fine. It almost hurts my boobs, but it feels exciting. I'm getting so hot. Now, I've readjusted it to pulse. That's the best. Oh God, so good."

Phil wrapped his hand around his cock and rubbed slowly.

"Now the spray is on my belly. It sort of tickles. I want to aim the spray at my pussy, but I'm deliberately holding back. It's nice to wait, to anticipate how that pulsing water will feel on my clit, on my lips, on my asshole."

Phil's hand moved faster.

"I can't wait any longer. I'm spraying my pussy now." Phil heard a long-drawn-out sigh. "That's wonderful. Not as good as your hands or your cock or, of course my favorite, your mouth. But what's a girl to do? God, it's good. I'm going to come without actually touching my snatch. Just this wonderful water. It just keeps pulsing, kneading my flesh. God, it's good. Just a little more."

Phil listened to the small animal noises his wife was making, knowing the sounds of her orgasm. For several long minutes, all he heard from the tape player were the sounds of the water and his wife's loud moans. "Yes," she hissed finally. "Yesssssss."

Phil suddenly stopped rubbing his cock, turned off the tape player, grabbed the phone, and dialed his home number. "Hello," Carol's soft voice said.

"Hi, darling," Phil said.

He heard Carol's giggle. "You're late. I expected your call an hour ago."

"I got lost trying to find this damned . . . What do you mean, you expected my call? We had agreed to cut down on the phone calls."

"You got my tape?"

Phil's smile widened. "Yes."

"Well, I just want you to know I'm lying here on the bed, without any clothes on. Would you like to know what I'm doing? Where my hand is right now?"

Phil began to stroke his cock again. "Yes, darling, you know I'd love to."

Stocking Stuffers

LISA FOUND the catalogue in the bathroom at her friend Carrie's house one early-December afternoon. "Do you really order stuff from this?" she asked when she returned to their Christmas decorating.

"Sure. We get a lot of catalogues. Rick and I paw through them, and just doing that gets us hot." She giggled. "Then we order a new toy or piece of lingerie and play again. Lord, it's fun."

"I would be so embarrassed," Lisa said.

"Yeah, we were, too, at first. But even the embarrassment is exciting." She winked at her friend. "You know, Christmas is coming. Take that catalogue. You could just stuff Ted's stocking with that. Think of the possibilities."

"Hmmm," Lisa said, putting the small slick-paper magazine in her purse. "Yeah. Think of that."

Later that evening, after Ted fell asleep, Lisa thumbed through the catalogue, her eyes widening as she gazed at the items for sale. As she turned the pages, her pulse speeded up, her breathing quickened, and her pussy moistened. After she closed the booklet, she climbed into bed beside Ted, woke him by nibbling on his neck, then fucked him senseless.

"What was that all about?" Lisa's husband asked when he caught his breath.

"Oh, nothing. I just wanted you."

"Well, whatever caused that 'nothing', bottle it."

"Ummm, yeah," Lisa mumbled as she fell asleep.

The following afternoon, Lisa again browsed the catalogue, found three items she wanted to buy for Ted's stocking, and called the company's 800 number. Contrary to her fears, the ordering process was simple and impersonal. The items she had ordered arrived in an unmarked package a few days later, and she quickly hid them in the back of her closet.

On Christmas morning, Ted and Lisa's three children filled the house with whoops of glee as they unwrapped their treasures. There were presents from the kids to their parents, and nice, practical gifts from each parent to the other.

Throughout the day, Lisa found her thoughts wandering to the items she had carefully gift wrapped and returned to the closet for later. Fortunately for Lisa's patience, the children dropped into bed, exhausted, early that evening.

The two parents cleaned up the family room and finally went upstairs. "Honey," Lisa said, her heart pounding, "I've got a few more presents for you."

"You have?" Ted said, puzzled. "I loved the sweater, and that new fishing gear was just what I wanted."

"I'm glad you liked what I got you, but I think you'll like these, too."

"I don't have anything else for you," Ted said, looking chagrined.

"You will," Lisa said with a grin as she led Ted into the bedroom. "Hook the door." She felt a bit nervous giving Ted such explicit presents, but the idea excited her sufficiently that she managed to fetch the gifts despite her trembling hands.

Ted placed the hook into the bracket so the children wouldn't be able to enter unannounced. Lisa motioned him to the bed, and he sat on the edge. Then she put three carefully wrapped boxes in his lap and sat down beside him. She handed him the smallest one. "This one first."

Ted tore the Christmas wrap and stared at the box that was revealed. "Slick-um Lubricant," the printing exclaimed. "Slipperiest water-based gel available."

He pulled out the jar and held it up. "Neat idea," he said, his voice neutral.

"Just for fun," Lisa said.

"Okay," Ted said, opening the second package. "Deep-Stroking Dildo with Clitoral Stimulator," the second package said. "You're kidding," Ted said. "You got me a dildo?"

Lisa was suddenly not sure she had done the right thing. Maybe Ted would take the gifts as some negative comment on his lovemaking. "It's just a toy," she said, her voice now small and weak. "It's for us. I thought we could play sometime." Her voice trailed off.

"I think it's a great idea," Ted said, staring at his wife. "I just never thought you'd be interested in stuff like this." He reached over and quickly hugged her. "Fan-flippin'-tastic."

The grin that spread across his face was reward enough for Lisa. It had been very scary, but it was going to be worth it. She picked up the third package. "I don't know whether this will be your thing," she said, "but the idea turned me on." Then she giggled. "Remember that night a few weeks ago? I had just found this in the catalogue."

"Oh," Ted said. "Oh!" He tore at the wrapping and saw a strange butterfly-shaped device. "Venus Butterfly," the box proclaimed. He read the explanation. "Did you get batteries?"

"They're included," Lisa said.

"Yeah." Ted fiddled with the heavy, two-inch in diameter, hot-pink plastic object and attached control box until he had the battery installed. "This is very interesting. Let's see just how it works," he said, a slightly professorial tone creeping into his voice. "Take your pants off." His leer belied his attempt to sound uninvolved.

Trembling with excitement and a bit of fear, Lisa removed her jeans and panties. As she started to unbutton her shirt, Ted took her hands. "For this to be a true test of how this thing works, I think we should have no additional stimulation. Lie down."

Lisa stretched out on the bed. The butterfly was attached to two elastic straps. "I think these go around your thighs," Ted said, slipping the loops around Lisa's feet and sliding them up her legs. He pulled the loops high on her hips so the butterfly pressed against her already wet pussy.

"Yipe, that's cold," Lisa said. Against her sizzling clit, it felt especially frigid.

"I'm really sorry about that," Ted said. He held a small plastic box that was connected to the butterfly with a slender wire. "Let's see whether this heats it up a bit." Lisa watched as Ted pushed a slide control with his thumb. "Oh God," she squealed as the item between her legs started to hum. "Oh shit, that's bad." She could feel the vibrations through her body, making her nipples suddenly erect and her back arch. "That's wicked," she puffed. "Oh God."

"Mmmm," Ted purred, stretching out beside her, rubbing a finger over one erect nipple. "I like what this does to you." He played with the slider, speeding then slowing the vibrations. Then he leaned over and lightly bit the nipple that reached for his mouth.

The butterfly caused a deep hunger to blossom in Lisa's body. She wanted, needed to be filled. "Fuck me," she said.

"Not so fast," Ted said. "Just lie there and don't move. Let this baby do its worst."

"But I want you now," Lisa moaned.

"Not yet." Ted continued to play with the control, watching his wife's face flush and her head thrash back and forth. Sensing that she was getting close, he stood up and quickly removed his pants and shorts. In the still-rational part of his mind, he thought, It was very brave of Lisa to buy this stuff and suggest something new. Maybe I could, too. He lay back beside his wife, slowed the vibrations, then took her hand. He placed it against his hard cock and wrapped her fingers around it. "Stroke me," he said, his voice hoarse.

Lisa was only too happy to squeeze his cock and move her hand from the base to the tip. Suddenly she wanted to take him into her mouth, something she hadn't done in a long time. The device still quietly humming against her clit, she opened her eyes, slid downward on the bed, and looked at Ted. She held his cock near her face and smiled.

"Oh yes," he groaned. "Do it."